STRANGE NOIR

Arthur Jett

ISBN
978-1-957378-63-3 (Paperback)
978-1-957378-62-6 (eBook)
978-1-957378-64-0 (Hardcover)

ACKNOWLEDGEMENT

*First of all, I would like to thank God.
I like to thank Linda for her great editing ability. And I
also like to thank Community Secretarial - Danielle, Sandy,
McKenzie, and last but not the least, Autumn.
Again, I want to thank God and for all the
great staff at Quantum Discovery.*

TABLE OF CONTENTS

Murder Follows Me

ARTHUR C JETT

TABLE OF CONTENTS

CHAPTER ONE

HE WAS AWAKE, he thought, barely. Couldn't see. A bloody hand came into focus. It was his hand. His head felt like it was splitting open. That was because it was. Blood flowed in his eyes. Where was he, and what had happened now?

His name was Johnny R. Jacks, but everyone called him Roary. He ran a detective agency that specialized in finding missing persons or spying on your husband or getting your cat out of a tree, whichever paid the most, or, in his case, paid at all.

Jacks Detective Agency had been around about ten years. Yes, high hopes on a small budget. It had been a downhill run for the last twelve years since Kitty had been murdered and Johnny R. Jacks had been a second-grade detective with the Los Angeles Police Department. After the Kitty Elaine Jacks case went into the cold case files, the department had to carry Roary for about a year before finally, with the drinking and all the misery that accompanied it, the department was forced to fire J. Roary Jacks.

Six months later, Roary climbed out of the bottle long enough to start Jacks Detective Agency. The agency was a small office with two rooms and a restroom down the hallway. It was located in the old Beverly Towers in North Hollywood. Roary had thought that Hollywood would be the place for some high-profile cases. But as it turned out, he was in a low-rent, low-budget, and seedy part of town. Lucky for Roary Jacks, the owner of the Beverly Towers was his old friend—well, okay, as much of a friend that Roary would allow himself to have—along with the lobby clerk, the head doorman, and sometimes the maintenance man. Roary also had employed thirty-five-year-old Maxine Winters, a single mother of a little girl named Chrissy, a know- it-all eight-year-old. Maxine took calls, ran the computer, and paid the bills when there was money.

CHAPTER TWO

HE PUSHED HIMSELF up. In the sitting position, he reached back in his back pocket, pulled out his handkerchief, and wiped away the blood. Then he held it there to try and stop the bleeding but not much luck. Surveying the room, it did not look familiar, but he was still pretty dizzy. The sun was bright in the room. Finally, he got to one knee and then up to standing. Now he could see what looked like an apartment. The front door was open. It looked like there had been a struggle or fight of some sort. The end table, lamp, and big chair were turned over with some books thrown about as if someone had been looking for something.

As he started for the door, he noticed something dark on the kitchen floor. It appeared to be blood, and the trail led down the hallway to the bedroom. The first thing he saw was a body beside the bed—a young woman, early twenties maybe. There was so much blood it was hard to tell. Not much of the room was not covered in it. It was hard to believe that much blood came from one person. It had taken a long time to bleed her out like that. The young woman had been stabbed multiple times, too many holes to count right offhand. The body had been mutilated. Along with having her throat cut, her eyes and ears were missing.

Roary had seen this work before. It was in Vietnam, in 1975, Saigon, where he had been a courier for the NIS, the Navy Intelligence Service. It was not the first time he had seen it here either. It was when he was a rookie with the LAPD and again as a detective, one of his first cases as a matter of fact.

Roary started out of the apartment when two uniformed police officers yelled, "Hands in the air! Down on your knees! Now! Do it!"

Roary knew the routine and gently fell to his knees and then to his belly, hands and arms out. The first officer pulled Roary's arms back behind him and then put the handcuffs on.

"Just lay there and take it easy, buddy. This is for your protection as well as ours."

The first patrolman made his way into the apartment. The second officer stood as guard at the front door. The first officer reappeared.

"Call for backup and get homicide out here."

Within minutes, the place was crawling with cops, detectives, and a portable lab. Along with all that came a news helicopter, a news reporter, and a crowd of about seventy-five to a hundred lookie-loos, those with mundane lives or a sense of the macabre.

Roary scanned the crowd and the surrounding area to try and make some sense of what had happened. Soon, a face that Roary recognized was opening the back door of the patrol car. It was Lt. First Grade Frank Gonzales, LA Metro Division Detective, Roary's old division back in the '80s and '90s.

"Roary? What the hell happened here?"

Roary shook his head. "Really don't know, Frank. I came to in the apartment, looked in the bedroom, and was making my way out when the uniforms showed up."

"Okay, Roary, we're going to get you to the hospital and get you sewed up."

"Frank, you seen this before?"

"Yes, but you're still going to have to come downtown. Your old buddy Captain Martin is going to want to talk to you."

"Oh great. First, I get my head split open. Then I get to go downtown and get my ass kicked by him."

CHAPTER THREE

WHILE AT THE hospital, several more junior-grade detectives asked a lot of questions. But the answers would be the same—"Don't know what happened" or "Don't know how I got there, who hit me, or who had killed the girl." It was getting late in the afternoon, four fifteen, and ten stitches later before Roary reached downtown to LA Metro and then upstairs to Capt. Greg Martin's office but not before Roary walked through the detective squad room. It looked about the same but modern. All eyes were on him, looking for any clue. Roary knew because it was what he would do.

"All right, Detective Gonzales, take off the cuffs."

"Yes, sir."

"Sit down, Roary," Captain Martin said with a bit of a growl in his tone. "You want to tell me what happened, Roary? But before you do, we found your car about a half a block away from the victim's apartment. The lab has it in impound."

Greg Martin had been a rookie a year or so behind Roary at the Police Academy. They had worked East LA and Pico Rivera in the late '80s together—rough neighborhoods, rough cops. Martin had always been ambitious but fair and had his eyes on bigger and better things, not always the people. Greg Martin had always wanted to be chief of police in Los Angeles County and probably would be if not for the necklace murders. That was what it was called in the '80s and '90s and even now, thirty years later. It was called the necklace murders because it was figured out that the murderer was cutting the ears off to make a necklace, the way they did in Vietnam in the '60s and '70s.

In late '89, Greg and Roary were on a routine call in the Monterey Park just off the Seventeen Freeway. They had stopped the patrol car across from the address that they received from dispatch. It was quiet, and no lights were on. They had gone to the front of the house. The door was open. They identified themselves as police officers and made their way in. They had called in for backup. They had a sense that something was very wrong. As they went through the living room, two shots rang out. The first hit Roary's Kevlar vest center mass. The second shot hit him just below the vest on his right side, just a flesh wound. The force sent him backward ten feet or so. Greg had turned and run out the front door for cover, and he didn't blame him. He would have done the same if he could have. The murderer made it out the back and a clean getaway.

The next thing he remembered was Greg yelling, "Roary, are you okay?"

Which he wasn't and had to be taken to LA County Hospital, where all he needed was a patch-up job. The bullet had just grazed his side. That all might sound bad, but he considered it the most luckiest night of his life. That was where he met Kitty. She was working the night shift and became his nightingale. Kitty was a twenty-eight-year-old RN with beautiful blond hair like spun gold and blue sapphire eyes as blue as he had ever seen, stood five feet nine inches, and had a body that would stop a rock star. Her brooding red lips were so full he often wondered how so much lip could still be so beautiful. She was smart as they came and funny. He couldn't tell how many times she had made him cry from laughing out loud. They talked on and off most of the night. He knew right away he had found his soul mate.

The next few days were spent healing up, but he didn't even notice. Once he had left the hospital, she was at his place, caring for him. After two months, he asked her to marry him.

She asked, "What took you so long?" And her reply was "Yes, I would love to marry you."

One month later, they were married. Life was good. They bought a house in the Valley to start their family. Soon after, he took the LAPD detective test and was promoted to the rank of second-grade detective. The extra money was good. Kitty and he had been married three and a half years when she found out they were pregnant. To think two people could be so happy, it was like they were living a dream. An extra shift at work was helping to pay the bills. She would grab an extra shift now and then to get money to save up for the soon-to-be-here baby Jacks.

It was Friday, around 7:00 p.m. When Roary got home, Kitty was working in someone's spot for just an extra hour. He called her and asked if she needed him to come and pick her up.

"Don't be silly," she said. "I have my car here. I will be home around ten. Don't wait up for me. You need your rest for work the next day. I'll be fine."

"Okay. I love you, darling."

At 5:15 a.m., he received a call from the hospital saying he needed to come there as soon as possible, that his wife had been hurt in a shooting. They lived five minutes from the hospital. When he arrived, he went straight to the emergency room. They said she was not there but in the parking garage. His mind was wanting to shut down. None of this made any sense to him. If she had been shot, why weren't they working on her? As fast as he could go, he ran to the parking garage. There were a lot of police cars and a crowd of people. Pushing his way through them, he yelled, "Kitty!" But as soon as he saw her, he knew she was gone. As best as he could recall, he fell to his knees and picked her in his arms. She was so limp and cold. She had been lying there since last night. Someone tried to pull him from her.

I screamed, "no! no!" and held her tighter.

A voice said, "You have to let her go. She's already gone. We need to get her inside now and let them take her. Patrolman Gonzalez will drive you home, Roary."

"What happened here!" he yelled.

"Carjacking's the best we can tell you right now, Roary."

Carjacking took the most beautiful thing in the world away from him, that and his child too, for a car. A white flash of rage was sent through his mind; his heart felt as if it were being twisted out of his chest. Something inside him didn't know it then, but he knew now. He would never be the same. He couldn't because the best part of him had just been shot in the head and had been whisked off to the morgue.

There had been no clues in the case. His car was found in West Hollywood on a rundown street two days later. Her purse and keys were still on the car's floorboard. Blood spatters, brain fragments, and hair were still on the roof. That was all the evidence. Nobody saw her head or anything. Nothing was found in the car. It was clean. A door-to-door investigation was conducted. For a four-block radius, again, nobody saw or heard anything, and after a month, it went to cold case file officially. But he couldn't let it go. For the next six months, he pounded that hospital and neighborhood for answers, but they didn't come. So he turned to the bottle to try and get the things his mind had seen out, but they would never be out, just forgotten for a short span of time. Then by not going to counseling and missing so much work, the department was forced to fire him. The bottle became his work for the next five years.

CHAPTER FOUR

ONE DAY ROARY looked out from the bottle of cheap wine. He had been through all his money from the sale of his home. Looking across from him was a storefront in a hotel, the Beverly Towers. The drink had taken its toll, but something inside him said *enough*. Walking across the street into the lobby, he could see small businesses all around—a coffee shop, a beauty shop, a newsstand. Nothing grand, just small mom-and-pop joints. Looking down the hill, there were small businesses, offices for an accountant, and an employment agency.

So he went to the front desk and inquired about office space for a private investigator. Of course, he would have to clean up and take the test and renew his gun permit. No big thing. He was motivated for the first time in five years. There was still life insurance money that he had not touched, couldn't 'til now. Kitty was lost, and this might help him find her killer. This was what he thought. So for the next few years, he righted the ship and turned things around for himself. His office was small, but it got the job done. Before too long, there were enough jobs to keep him busy, in fact, so busy he was thinking about getting a girl Friday to come in and tidy up the place, maybe do some light typing and answer the phone. It was 1998, and there were barely any cell phones. Unless you carried a shoebox around with you and then they rarely worked—people would look like they were a member of a drug cartel. Who knew that cell phones would change who we were as a society?

One of the first jobs that Jacks Detective Agency received was from the owner of the Beverly Towers, a Mr. Oliver Rosenberg. Now Oliver was in his late 40s, 5'6" tall, 160 pounds, slightly built, and a real estate entrepreneur with holdings throughout Los Angeles and along the coast of California. Oliver was a very shrewd businessman who bought and sold properties like fruit at a farmer's market. Oliver had a home out in

Malibu—a sprawling five-acre estate with a pool, a tennis court, and a ten-million-dollar view of the Pacific Ocean and a sandstone beach house. Yes, Oliver did pretty good for himself. Oliver's first wife died four years ago in 1994 in a car crash along Pacific Coast Highway, south of Monterey. She had been on a trip to buy some property because that was what she and Oliver did, always trying to one-up each other. Kind of a game they played, Oliver told Roary. It had been raining, and there had been a rockslide that brought traffic to a standstill. With the roads being wet, she didn't stop in time and was killed instantly.

Three years later, Oliver married a woman half his age, a Ms. Suzy Boneich, a poster girl for party girls in 1990—the big hair, short shirt, big boots, Madonna look-alike. Oliver had fallen head over heels for her, and why not? She was a knockout. The two of them threw big parties on a regular basis and hobnobbed with society's cream of the crop—showbiz types, actors, producers, directors. Hell, Oliver knew Oliver Stone, Al Pacino, and the list went on. Six months into the party, Oliver started to notice this and that, pretty boys hanging around. Suzy was taking little trips to Las Vegas for a couple of days or a weekend with her gal pals. Sometimes they would go to San Francisco for a weekend to get away. Suzy began to spend a lot of Oliver's money. Oliver had set up an account for her needs—$500,000. It was gone in a matter of months. Now for Oliver, jealousy was getting the better of him. The honeymoon was over. And the romance was gone, at least for Oliver.

Oliver had seen Roary's sign hanging in the lobby of the Beverly Towers and came in to see him. Oliver introduced himself. It was about ten o'clock on a Tuesday morning, not much was going on, and in walked Oliver Rosenberg.

"You Jacks?"

"Detective Jacks. Yes, may I help you?"

"My name is Oliver Rosenberg, and I own this place. Yes, it's about my wife, my young wife. Suzy may be more than I bargained for."

He struck Roary as a timid man, someone not wanting to rock the boat. You could tell he cared about Suzy and that he did not want to be here talking to him about her.

"I just need to know, Mr. Jacks."

"Call me Roary, and what is it you need to know?"

"Well"—he hung his head—"I need to know if she's being faithful to me."

"Okay, Mr. Rosenberg."

"Please call me Oliver."

"Oliver, I charge two hundred a day plus expenses."

"That will be fine, Roary. Here is a photo of my wife. My home address is on the back, and here's my business card with my numbers. Roary, I need you to be *discreet*."

"All right, Oliver. I will be contacting you with my report."

Oliver looked around the office and said, "Don't you have a secretary here?"

"No need for one yet. Business is slow. No, I just got a big job."

He smiled. "Ya, I guess you do."

They stood and shook hands, and Oliver left. It occurred to Roary that he was his landlord and that he better not screw it up. What was the crack about the secretary?

Two days later, at a club outside Malibu on Highway 1 called Breaker, Suzy Boneich Rosenberg made her first stop of the night. Suzy had told Oliver that she was going out to meet an old girlfriend who had just got in town and was at her cousin's place and asked Suzy to come over and visit a while. Suzy assured Oliver he would be bored out of his mind. Being a private investigator (PI) meant being there but not being seen or noticed. So at first, Roary stayed on the other side of the club, where Suzy was meeting a friend, but he was not a girl. The two right away got real friendly, and after a few cocktails, they left the club. The low-light spy cam that was used to take a still photo was a handy little tool. But it might have been too dark inside the club for it to be any good. In the parking lot, Suzy and her male companion locked lips in a very passionate kiss and got into Suzy's '98 SL 500 Mercedes-Benz red convertible, a wedding present from Oliver after the honeymoon in Hawaii. Suzy was making his job very easy.

His little Toyota Camry was complete with Sony camcorder, coffee thermos, Nikon camera with a 30-1 zoom lens for more still shots, and hyperbolic microphone good for almost fifty yards. It was so good it was like you were sitting right next to them on the seat. There was also a new box of Hostess doughnuts because on a stakeout, you need to keep up your strength. And since he had quit drinking, they had become his favorite.

Suzy and her male friend pulled the SL out onto the highway and started up the coast. They had traveled three miles when the SL 500 pulled into a small motel called the Ocean Breeze. The two checked in, went to their room, and were inside for the next two hours. There was nothing to do but wait.

By 7:30 p.m., Suzy and her male counterpart emerged from their room and got into the Benz and went back to the club, where Suzy, after another couple of deep kisses, left her male companion and returned to her home in Malibu. Oliver was right in his suspicion.

The next day, Suzy had an appointment with her hairdresser in Beverly Hills, an off Rodeo Drive salon called Fab Mackie's. Her appointment was for 2:00 p.m. Oliver had given Roary Suzy's itinerary for the next day. So he followed the SL across town; it was a snap. She had parked her car in the back parking lot of Mackie's salon and walked in the front of the building. Doing a walk-by with the Sony camcorder slung over his shoulder with a carrying strap, this would get shots of what was going on inside, and it was just as he thought. Several women and men were busily making over costumers, eight to ten people in the small shop.

After the walk-by, Roary went to his car and studied the camcorder. It showed Suzy sitting and getting her hair done. An hour went by. Suzy and her hairdresser went out to the Mercedes and got in. But they did not leave. Using the Nikon with the zoom lens, it was easy to tell that they were engaging in drug use. The couple spent a few minutes putting the dope up their noses, and then they kissed a few times. Then even to his surprise, Suzy began to give her friend a blow job right in broad daylight. Suzy was very photogenic, and Roary supposed she really liked her hairdo.

CHAPTER FIVE

IT HAD ONLY been a couple of days, and already, the evidence was overwhelming. Suzy had gotten Roary in with Oliver good. Over the next few years, there were cases that had ranged from people stealing from their companies to corrupt business partner in the movies. Yes, a lot of indiscretions from a lot of powerful people.

After showing the video to Oliver, he turned it over to his lawyer and was able to get an annulment. Oliver, the kind soul he was, sent Ms. Suzy packing with a half a million dollars in her purse. Three months later, she was killed in a cocaine robbery gone wrong.

Being a PI, you see things like this because you examine people's lives up close on a daily basis for hours on end. And in all his years watching, nobody just sat still. They pricked their fingers, they bumped their heads, they tripped and fell. They did good things like opening the door for somebody else. They said things like "Oh, excuse me, did you drop this?" The good usually outweighed the mean or the outright evil. "Get out of my way, stupid." "See, look what you have done, moron." "I will tear your head off."—these were the things they said and did on a regular basis, but most of them didn't have a clue what was going on so very close to them and if even himself. A lot of the time, they were so focused on their jobs or day-to-day activities or just within themselves that huge occurrences happened right in front of them and they didn't hear or see. But sometimes they were surprised or startled and even scared by the fabric of life as they treaded through it, pushing and dodging, shoving or just standing in it, and letting it pass us by, most of the time unaware.

Oliver Rosenberg wasn't one to miss a lot. After Suzy's untimely and unfortunate demise, Oliver had called Roary and wanted to see him in his office. Oliver kept an office in the penthouse of the Beverly Towers. Over the years, Oliver and Roary developed a pretty good friendship. So sometimes they would just talk about things—what star was sleeping with which star, what mover and shaker was making a move, who's buying a house or making a movie, who's cheating on who with who. As he made his way into his office, he met Oliver's new secretary, young Ms. Donna Gates, smart enough not to be Oliver's flavor of the month.

"Hello, Mr. Jacks. The boss is expecting you."

"Donna, just call me Roary, please."

With a half-cocked smile, she said, "Okay, Roary," as she kind of did a wiggle in her seat as he entered Oliver's large, oversized thousandsquare-foot office. He was sitting behind an equally large—best he could tell—ebony wood desk with a hand-carved depiction of a frontier cross wagon oxen, that sort of thing.

"Hi, Roary. Come in and sit down."

"What's going on, Oliver?"

"Well, something is bothering me about the pictures you took of Suzy."

"Oh yeah? What's that?"

"Here, let me show you. Since she was killed, I was sort of missing her and looking at the pictures. Just feeling a little guilty, I guess. But here, look at these."

"What am I looking for, Oliver?"

"This guy right here." He pointed to a man in the background that *appeared* to be looking directly at the couple in the car or over the car, looking at the camera.

"Yeah, so what? He is a bystander."

"Yeah, that's what I thought, but here, look at the pictures from the Ocean Breeze motel, the room next to the one Suzy and her boyfriend are coming out of."

Roary looked at the picture and saw the man standing in the window, looking out as if to look at the camera.

"Isn't that the same guy?"

"I don't know, Oliver. He is not in focus in either shot. But it does look like the same guy."

"That's what I thought. Now look at the video you brought me. Look as you are walking by the front of the salon, recording what was going on inside. There! Behind you in the reflection of the glass. It's him."

Roary studied the recording almost in shock to see the man walking two steps behind him, looking in the shop as Roary was.

"Odd. I don't remember him being there, and as far as the picture goes, I'm not sure."

"It's him, Roary. Who is he?"

"I don't know, Oliver. It could just be a coincidence." But Roary felt the hair on the back of his neck stand.

"Well, it's probably nothing. I just thought it was odd."

"Yes, I have to agree. It kind of gives me the willies."

"Do you mind if I keep these? I don't keep copy of my work for professional reasons."

"Sure, Roary. I don't need to keep looking at those anyway. Oh yeah, this isn't the only reason I called you up here. My lawyer may have a job for you. If you're interested."

"Sure. I will give him a call."

"You want to grab some lunch, Roary?"

"No. Better get back to work. Pay the rent and all, you know."

As he left Oliver's office, he couldn't shake the feeling of being watched. As he passed Donna, it occurred to him about having a secretary. His office needed a bit of a woman's touch.

CHAPTER SIX

AT THE LAW offices of Reicher and Reicher, Roary waited in the receptionist area to present his findings on a long-running case he had been working on. It had been a big job that involved a larger talent agency, which holdings included television, billboard, and movie actors. If it had anything to do with media, they had a piece of the pie. What was happening in the new millennium? Was not all the computer crash just the opposite happened? They got stronger, faster, and smarter, but with that, the rewards of dishonesty skyrocketed. Even the best security was inept, and millions of dollars were being stolen from a number of accounts there out in the world. And the Insight Talent Agency was different. Everything was put into the computer. For example, if the agency was paid $235,000, then the 72$ would go into a numbers account of its own, one the accountant had the only access code to. Now 73$ doesn't sound like much, but when you are doing thousands of deals, it adds up pretty quick. It was pretty easy to notice for Roary and the heads of the agency, but proving it was something else. If the person or persons were alerted, they could erase or transfer the account to an offshore account. Insight's billboard revenues alone were upwards of $100 million a year.

The company CEO was Daryl Bainer, a Harvard graduate with an MBA degree. Daryl was a bit old school. He liked to look at the books, if you would. A condensed version was supplied every month. He had noticed a small discrepancy. All the accounts ended in roundoff numbers. He wasn't positive, but it looked like a new twist to an old scam. Roary had been on the case almost two years. It was a lot of money, close to $10 million, but Roary finally caught a break. An employee went on vacation to the Cayman Islands, a popular place to hide money, and he had gone twice. Now all that Roary had to do was monitor the computer station in which the perpetrator worked from, and bingo, there it was. Allen P.

Smithers was able to tap into all of Insight's accounts and transfer the money to his own account in the Caymans. Allen had outdone himself. All that money and he did not know what to do with it. There was much. He knew if he tried to spend it, he would be noticed. So he didn't spend, but he couldn't stop piling up. The problem was that Allen P. Smithers had no personality whatsoever. At first, it was exciting for Allen and even fun. But then Allen got scared. He had even thought about turning himself in with the money, and if he had, he may have still went to jail but not for long. But as it stood now, even with Insight getting almost all its money back, Allen P. Smithers could still do seven to fifteen years in jail for grand larceny. Roary was just wrapping up some loose ends for all his accounts.

"Mr. Bainer will see you now, Mr. Jacks."

"Thanks," Roary said and went in to Daryl Bainer's office.

"Hello, Roary. Have a seat. I will be with you in just a moment." Roary sat in the plush office.

"Can I get you something, Roary? Coffee, water, soft drink?"

"No, thanks, Daryl. I'm fine."

Daryl Bainer, big guy, smart, and pleasant enough, finished writing in a folder and closed it.

"Good to see you, Roary. You got something for me there?"

"Yes, these are my last expense reports hand delivered as you requested." Roary handed them to him. "You will find they are all in order, Daryl."

"Roary, I am sure they are. It was just an excuse to get you in here. Mrs. Collins, could you come in here?"

A few seconds later, his secretary appeared through the doors of the outer office. Daryl handed her Roary's file and the other file.

"Can you file these, please?"

"Yes, Mr. Bainer, I'll do it right away."

"And, Judy, can you bring me some coffee, please?"

"Yes. Would you like some coffee too, Mr. Jacks?"

"No, thanks."

"Okay, I'll be right back, Mr. Bainer."

"Roary, you have done an excellent job over the past two years and saved this company literally $10 million. We will pay your regular fees, Roary, and your expenses for a job well done." Daryl handed Roary a check for $250,000.

"Daryl, this isn't necessary."

"Oh yes, it is, and on top of that, we would like to keep you on retainer. What do you say, Roary?"

"Well, I suppose the only thing I can say is okay."

"Good, Roary. Glad to have you on board!"

"Thanks, Daryl. This means a lot to me and my company."

Roary was making a name for himself with Oliver Roseburg, Reicher and Reicher, and his biggest client of all, Insight Talent Agency. The bonus would come in handy. Roary could now afford a secretary and a new car. It really felt as if he might be okay. As long as he kept busy, things would work out. It was the first time in five years since Kitty had been murdered that he was alive, and she was just gone, not dead.

CHAPTER SEVEN

"MR. ROSEBURG, THERE is a call from Mr. Jacks on line 1." "Okay, Donna, I got it. Hello, Roary. I heard the great news from my attorney."

"Well, thanks, Oliver. The reason I am calling is Jacks Detective Agency needs a secretary, and I thought you might know someone that could help me out."

"Sure, Roary. When you hang up, I will have Donna get you the number. Say, why don't you come out to the house tonight? We'll throw a couple of steaks on and watch some football."

"That sounds good, Oliver. What time do you want me there?"

"Oh, six thirty or seven, if that is okay with you."

"Yeah. That sounds fine."

"Okay, see you there."

A few minutes later, Donna called from Oliver's office. She gave Roary the number to the temp agency where she had been hired on from. Soon, Roary had several applicants. The first couple of applicants did not match up with what Roary was looking for, but the third, a Ms. Maxine Winters, did. She was young, beautiful, smart, and hungry, a single mom with a baby daughter.

"Ms. Winters, you got the job, and you can start on Monday at 9:00 a.m. sharp."

"Thank you, Mr. Jacks."

"Please call me Roary, and I will see you on Monday."

"You won't regret hiring me, Roary. I will do a good job for you."

About that time, Bobby Clark came into the office. Bobby and Roary had gotten to be pretty good friends over the past five or six years.

"Hi, Roary. Is this your new secretary?"

"Why, yes, it is. Maxine Winters, meet Bobby Clark. He is the doorman here at the Beverly. If I am not here, he can show you the ropes here at the hotel."

"Oh, that would be nice, and good to meet you, Bobby."

"No, the pleasure is all mine, Ms. Winters."

"Oh, please call me Maxine."

"Very well, Maxine."

"Is there something I can help you with, Bobby?"

"Well, I will be leaving, Roary, so you can talk, and I will see you first thing on Monday morning."

"All right, Maxine, and thank you. What is it, Bobby?"

"Have you seen today's paper?"

"No, why?"

"Here, see for yourself." There on the front bottom of the Metro police page was the caption "The Neckless Murderer Is Back." "It seemed there had been at least two murders with the victims' eyes missing. One in San Pedro and the other was in Carson, California. Your friend Lieutenant Martin caught the case in Carson, and they were forming a task force." Bobby kept up on all police business in the newspaper. He liked thinking he was a junior detective. He was a better doorman, but he did keep Roary well informed about the goings-on of LA finest men in blue.

So hearing the neckless murderer was back in the business made Roary uncomfortable, to say the least. Roary always felt he knew more about the case than he did. He didn't know why, just a gut feeling, he thought. It had been almost thirty years since Vietnam, which is where the first neckless murder occurred. Roary's mind would automatically flash back to that day in 1975, just north of Saigon in a little village, where he and First Lt. C. Baker were called to investigate the murder of a young Vietnamese woman. Roary's job was to drive and take pictures of the scene. NIS had been called in because of the brutality and the proximity to Saigon. First Lt. Cake Baker was a tall, slim-built man. That was about all Roary could remember about him and that he was very thorough and smart. That was what Roary remembered, how very smart the lieutenant seemed to be, but that was it.

Roary had been out of the marines since 1979, and a lot of water had passed under the bridge—water and booze—a lot of it. Roary had been on a pretty good run for the past five years, but that was about to change.

"Thanks, Bobby. I will read the police blotter a little later."

"Roary, do you think the neckless murder is back in business two murders inside a week?"

"No, Bobby, I think the murder has always been in business, but something has agitated him."

"Do you think it would be a copycat murderer?"

Roary did not know the answer to that question, but he did know someone who did.

"No. I will have to get back to you on that one, Bobby."

CHAPTER EIGHT

ON JULY 7, 2002, about 1:30 p.m., hot as hell in LA that day, Roary walked into Metro headquarters, LAPD detective squad. Roary went to the sergeant's desk and asked to see Detective Martin, Roary's old patrol partner. Roary went to Detective Martin's cubicle.

"Hey, Roary, come on in and sit down. What can I help you with?"

It was what Martin said, but he already knew why Roary was there. "It's about the neckless murders."

"Look," Greg Martin interrupted Roary, "I can't tell you a thing about the case, Roary, and you know that."

"Come on, Greg, how long have you known me?"

"It doesn't matter, Roary. The police department needs to keep a lid on the facts of this one."

"Look, Martin, maybe I can help in some way."

"Roary, I am warning you! Stay out of police business! Especially this one!"

"Can you at least tell me if it's a copycat you are working on?"

"No!" Martin yelled loud enough for the whole precinct to hear. "Roary, go on back to chasing cheaters and leave the police work to the professionals. I mean it, Roary. I will lock you up if I find out that you have been messing around in this case."

Roary got up and walked out. He was mad, but he didn't say anything or knock Martin on his ass. Detective Martin's actions told Roary two things: one, the neckless murders were not copycats and two, Detective Martin had absolutely no clues in the case.

Roary's first step would be San Pedro, where the first murder victim had been found. The paper had said that the murder had occurred at a seedy little hotel called the Lighthouse, just off the pier on Hardor Street. Roary went in to see an old man behind the counter.

"My name is Jacks. Hear about the murders?"

"Second floor, room 202. I thought you cops were done here." "Just doing a little checking up. Were you on duty when it happened?" "Probably. I am the only one that is on duty here."

Roary looked around the small lobby. No one was there but one older guy reading the paper.

"Did you see or hear anything the night it happened?"

"No, don't know. Look, I told you cops everything I know. A young woman came in about four in the afternoon and rented the room."

Roary pulled out a notebook. "What was her name again?"

The clerk looked puzzled and said, "Here, look for yourself." He opened the register book and turned it around so Roary could read it for himself and pointed to a name, M. Jones.

"Yeah, we get a lot of M. Jones or J. Smith here."

The guy reading the paper laughed out loud.

"Mister, you think murder is funny?"

"No," the man said, "but Jones and Smith is. Wouldn't you agree?" "How about you? Did you see or hear anything?"

"No, I wasn't here. I was working." The man lowered his head back into the paper.

"You got a key to the room?"

"No, the police still have it."

Roary didn't need a key. He knew what it looked like—a young woman between eighteen and twenty-four years old, blood everywhere with her eyes cut out, her throat cut from ear to ear, or her ears not just cut off but cut from the bottom up, very clean and even. Maybe the dental work and fingerprints would turn up the girl's real identity, if the police were lucky. Roary made his way up to 4216 Sixty-Eighth St., Carson, where the second murder had occurred. It was a quiet middle-class neighborhood. The police tape was still up around the property—a small white house with a kept, nicely manicured front yard and a separate single-car garage. Both house and garage had a red Spanish tile roof, which is very common in South California.

As Roary walked up to the police tape, a woman on her porch said, "Are you a reporter?"

Roary answered, "Why, yes, ma'am, I am."

"It's a shame what happened to that poor young woman, and it just as well could have been me."

Roary thought, *Except you are forty years too old.*

"We haven't had a break-in in this neighborhood for years, not even a barking dog. Mary buys a house. A month later, she is dead."

"Mary . . . Her name was Mary?"

"Yes, Mary Jones. She worked for a talent company or something like that."

"You mean a talent agency?"

"Yes, that talent agency, somewhere in Hollywood or Beverly Hills. She loved that little old house. What paper did you say you were from?"

Roary ignored her question as if he hadn't heard her. "Did Mary have a car?"

"Yes, the police took it, put it on a big truck, tow truck with a flatbed."

"Do you know what time the police think it might have happened?"

"Two nights ago. Nobody around here heard or seen anything, or I would have heard about it. The police went up and down the street, asking all kinds of questions."

"What's your name, ma'am, if you don't mind me asking?"

"You are not going to put it in the paper, are you? Because I wouldn't want that maniac coming after me."

"No, I would not put it in the paper, reporter confidentiality. You . _ . . _ " are my source.

"Well, in that case, my name is Jenny, Jenny Smith."

Roary's mind began to race. The name on the register was M. Jones, and the guy made the joke about it. "We get a lot of M. Jones and J. Smith."

"Jenny, I have to go. You have been very helpful." Roary turned and started running for his car.

The old woman yelled out, "What paper do you work for?"

CHAPTER NINE

ROARY WAS FLYING through traffic a lot faster than he should have been. He had made it back to San Pedro to the Lighthouse Hotel in less than thirty minutes. As Roary turned on to Harbor St., a black-and-white car was turned in the opposite direction, and Roary hit them dead center. Roary was semiconscious. He could hear people yelling. It was the police.

"Are you all right? What's the matter with you? Are you drunk?" "No!"

"Why are you driving like an idiot? You could have killed us! Let's see your driver's license."

"Killer inside. There is a killer inside. That's why I was driving like that. There is a killer inside the hotel."

"What the hell are you talking about?"

"The girl who was killed here two nights ago. I was talking to her killer earlier in the lobby. Look, I'm an ex-cop. I just figured it out, and I was coming back for him."

"All right, just settle down, buddy."

The officer called for backup. "Yes, Metro, this is Adam 51. We have a 10-33 auto accident with a police car involved, and be informed, a possible homicide suspect, 10-4."

"Did you say homicide suspect in custody—10-4?"

"Yes, 10-4, Metro. Copy that. Our location is the Lighthouse Hotel down on Harbor St., San Pedro."

"Copy, 51. Do you need an ambulance?"

"Yeah, better send one."

"Copy that, 51."

"Hey," Roary yelled, "the guy could be getting away!"

"All right, relax. What does he look like?"

"Well, I don't know exactly. He was sitting down with a newspaper in front of his face."

Roary had blood running down the side of his head where he had hit it on the steering wheel.

The officer took him by the arm. "You better come over here and sit down till the medic gets here."

"Yeah," Roary said, "I think you're right. I don't feel so good, partner."

The second officer spoke. "I am not feeling so hot either. All right, you two sit down over here on the curb." By this time, there was a crowd beginning to build.

"Okay, I am going to go inside and see who is who in the lobby." Roary and the second cop, whose name was Loas J. Alizara, sat on the sidewalk curb.

A man in the crowd handed Roary half his T-shirt. "You better put this on the cut on your head to stop the bleeding." The other half of the shirt he handed to Officer J. Alizara, who had a pretty good mouse under his right eye that was bleeding. Backup and the ambulance arrived. The first officer was advising back on what was happening, and the three of them went into the lobby. The medic attended to their injuries.

"You will both have to go to the hospital to get stitched up." As Roary and Officer J. Alizara were getting in the ambulance, Officer M. Kawarski returned from the hotel.

"Are you all right, Johnny?"

At the same time, Roary and Johnny Alizara said, "Yeah."

Roary looked at Officer Alizara and said, "My name is Johnny too."

The manager said he didn't know the guy in the lobby with the newspaper, said that he thought he was a guest but could not remember him exactly. He said there had been an officer there earlier but never said he was a cop.

The medic said, "We need to get them to the hospital."

"Okay. I will be right behind you, Johnny."

The two in the ambulance looked at each other, and Officer Alizara said, "All right, partner."

On the way, the two made small talk. "Sorry about your face," Roary exclaimed.

"It's all a part of the job. What about you? How come you're not a cop anymore, and what's the line on this murder suspect you were going on about?"

"Well, Johnny, long story short, my wife was murdered in a carjacking. Never did find the murderer. And I spent five years in the bottle. Been clean about four years. Got my PI business, the Johnny R. Jacks Agency. Been doing pretty good too. The murderers go way back."

"The neckless murderer?"

"Yeah, that's right. You have heard of them?"

"Kind of hard not to, being LAPD."

"Yeah, I guess that you're right."

"So do you think that was him in the lobby earlier?"

"Yeah, I do."

He made a joke about the murder in Carson. When the ambulance arrived at LA County General, Det. Greg Martin was waiting.

CHAPTER TEN

JACKS, I WARNED you to stay out of this. Now I have an injured patrol officer, a wrecked patrol car, and a murder investigation that has probably been compromised."

"Sir, he may have information pertinent to your case."

"All right, Officer, but you go get treated, and have your report on my desk tomorrow, okay?"

"Yes, sir."

The young Johnny Alizara was taken on back into the emergency room. "As for you, Roary, I will see you tomorrow down at Metro! Officer Kawarski!"

"Yes, sir."

"I want you to stay here till the hospital is done with Mr. Jacks here. Then take him down to Metro and book him for reckless driving. Got it?"

"Yes, sir."

"Wait a minute, Detective Martin!" Roary said. "That was the reckless murderer in the lobby today. Greg, he made a joke about the murder in Carson. The only way he would have known the initials to both M. Jones at the hotel and J. Smith, the next-door neighbor to the murder victim in Carson, was if he was there."

He laughed about it.

"Greg, and if Mary Jones was murdered in Carson, who was murdered in San Pedro at the Lighthouse Hotel?"

"That is none of your business, Roary! You're not a cop anymore, and you were warned. Now you're going to jail."

"Who was she, Martin?"

"All right, Roary. She was an actress from the Insight Talent Agency. Her name was Melody Johnston. We think she was working or moonlighting. That is all we know. Now what do you know about the guy with the newspaper?"

"Nothing. I didn't get a good look, but I would say fiftyish, tall, maybe six feet four inches, kind of a deep voice. Now that I think about it, he sounded kind of familiar."

"What do you mean?" the detective asked.

"Just familiar. Can't place it."

Roary didn't tell Greg Martin that he also worked for Insight Talent Agency. He figured he would do some digging around at the agency first. The next day, Roary paid his own bail and made his way to his office. As he walked in, there was his new secretary, Maxine Winters.

"Well, good morning, Roary!"

"Oh, good morning, Maxine."

"How are you?"

"I am fine."

"You look a little weathered."

"Yeah, I spent the night in jail. Wrecked my car yesterday, got charged with reckless driving, had to spend the night in jail."

"You had two phone calls this morning, one from Oliver Rosenburg and the other was Mr. Bainer from the Insight Talent Agency. He said to please call him. It was urgent."

"Okay, Maxine, get Mr. Bainer on the phone. I will be in my office."

"Okay, Roary. Would you like me to bring you some coffee?"

"Yes, please. That would be real nice. Thank you." Roary's back office had a restroom with a shower, and Roary kept an extra set of clothes there also.

"Mr. Bainer on the phone, Roary," the intercom blared.

"Okay, Maxine, I've got it."

"Hello, Mr. Bainer. What can I help you with?"

"Roary, not one but two of my employees turned up dead in the last two days."

"Yes, I am aware of that, Mr. Bainer. The police don't want me anywhere near those cases. As a matter of fact, I just got out of jail for poking my nose where it didn't belong, well, at least as far as the police are concerned. If it's all right with you, I would like to see if anybody might know something. Maybe something they saw or heard."

"It is okay with me, Roary. I would like to get to the bottom of this as soon as possible. It is real bad for business."

"Yes, I understand, Mr. Bainer, and I will be as discreet as possible."

"All right, Roary. Thank you."

"Goodbye."

With that, Roary began to get ready for his shower, when Maxine knocked on the door.

"Come in!"

"Here is your coffee, Roary."

"Just set in on my desk. Thanks, Maxine."

The tall redhead did as ordered and turned to walk away. Roary could not help but see how lovely she was—ivory pale skin, bright blue eyes, a chiseled nose, and high cheekbones. She was about five feet ten inches, Roary thought, and very full body. With years on the force, Roary usually noticed a lot of things about a person. Maxine had that part real easy. Maxine had been married to a college professor who was really into his students, especially the female ones. The marriage had only lasted one year. According to Maxine, it was about a year and a half too long. The only good thing to come of it was his two-year-old daughter.

Roary showered and got dressed and then called Oliver Rosenburg.

"Hello, Oliver. My secretary said you wanted me to call you."

"Hello, Roary. Are you here at the tower?"

"Yes, I am."

"Well, if you have a minute, can you come up to my office?"

"Yeah, sure. I will be right up."

"All right, good. I will see you then."

CHAPTER ELEVEN

ROARY WAS ON his way to the penthouse office at the Beverly Towers when he heard, "Where is your car at, Roary?" It was Bobby Clark. "I didn't see it out front where you usually parked."

Roary walked over to where Bobby was sitting by the main doors. "Had a major fender bender yesterday and totaled my car and a police cruiser."

"Are you all right?"

"Yeah. Just a few stitches. I am fine."

"What happened?"

"It's a long story, and I have to go up and see your boss right now."

"Sure. I understand. Did you read the police blog in the paper today?"

"No, why?"

"Seems there was another murdered police officer last night. He was strangled to death down at Metro last night. His name was Polowski, Kwowski. Something like that."

"Kowarski?"

"Yeah, I think that is it. I thought you said you didn't read the blog?"

Roary felt a cold sweat start to break out. "I didn't!" Roary made his way on up to Oliver's office.

"Hi, Roary. Oliver, I mean, Mr. Rosenburg is expecting you. Go on in."

"Thanks. Donna."

"Hello, Roary. Come on in and sit down."

"Kind of busy this morning, Oliver. What can I help you with?"

"All right, Roary, I will get right to the point. The girl that was murdered down at San Pedro a couple of nights ago, I knew. Do you know who I am talking about?"

"Yes, Oliver, I know who you are talking about. One Ms. Melody Johnston. And let me guess, you met her through the Insight Talent Agency."

"Man, you are good. Roary, how did you know that?"

"Well, let's just say I am beginning to see a pattern. What is your concern, Oliver? That you had a sexual encounter with Ms. Johnston and your young ex-wife just died a few months ago also?"

"Yeah, that's pretty much it."

"Don't think you have much to worry about, Oliver. Do you have an alibi for two nights ago?"

He hesitated for a moment.

"Yes, I do."

"But you don't want to tell me."

"That's right, but I have a feeling you know anyway, don't you, Roary?"

"Yes, you've been held up for the past few nights with your secretary, Donna, right here in the penthouse."

"Dang, Roary, do you know what color my underwear is?"

"No, Oliver, but I do know that the murders were committed by a serial killer, one that seems to be playing games with me."

"What makes you say that, Roary?"

"Because he is playing too close to the vest." Roary knew that the killer was trying to leave a trail for him, but how was he getting so close without Roary knowing? He didn't know for sure, but Roary would be watching closer.

Roary left Oliver and caught a cab to police headquarters. The sergeant at the front desk saw Roary coming and said, "Oh boy, not you again."

"Yeah, that's right, and I need to see Detective Martin."

The desk sergeant shook his head. "Okay, pal, it's your funeral. Have a seat." A few minutes later, Detective Martin appeared.

"Come on back, Roary." The two men made their way into the detective squad room.

"You know why I am here, right, Greg?"

"Yeah, to pay for the police car you wrecked."

Roary said, "That too, I suppose. Did you get video of Kowarski murdered?"

"You just can't stay out of police business, can you, Roary? You know if you hadn't been in jail last night when it happened, I would arrest you for the murder."

"Look, Martin, whoever the murderer is, I think he is trying to set me up, and I am only here trying to help."

"Okay, Roary, maybe you're right, and yes, we do have some video of the murder. It took place in the underground parking lot but not of the whole thing, just the initial attack. Come on, follow me."

The two made their way into an office that looked like an editing room for a TV station.

"All right, here it is." The detective hit the Play button. The video showed Kowarski opening the trunk of his car, when all of a sudden, an arm was thrown around his neck and locked on. Roary's eyes widened as he watched the officer struggle for his life. Within seconds, it was over. The officer and the murderer were out of sight of the camera.

"Greg, I know that move. It's taught to marines in basic training, or at least it was twenty-five years ago."

"There is more, Roary." They walked back to Detective Martin's desk, where he found the photos of Kowarski's body. "It was arranged."

"What do you mean?"

"It was placed in a certain position. Here, look for yourself."

Roary looked at the picture in disbelief. He could feel the blood leaving his head and his knees starting to buckle. The photos showed a man lying on the ground in a sort of running position. This was not the first time Roary had seen this. It was the same position Kitty was in when she was shot in the head and carjacked. Roary had thought she must have landed that way. But it was right there in the photo exactly as it was with Roary's beloved Kitty. There was no doubt in Roary's mind the killer was the same one who had killed Kitty.

"Are you all right, Roary? You don't look so good."

The photo was more than Roary's mind could handle.

"Roary, sit down!"

"No, I have to go."

"Okay, Roary, let me have one of the patrol officers take you home."

"No, I can get there on my own."

Roary made it as far as the first bar he came to. For the next four years, Roary would be in and out of the nearest bar he could find. His friends tried to help, but it was no use. The thought of Kitty's death was somehow his fault and would haunt him for the rest of his days. For the four years the murders had stopped, or at least it seemed like they stopped, Roary managed to keep working somehow, mostly stakeouts for a jilted lover or a cheating spouse, but he was never in good shape, never good enough for corporate espionage work, so the big money went away. Oliver let him keep his office for next to nothing, and Maxine's loyalties proved to be a godsend for Roary. She was the driving force behind Jacks Detective Agency, by keeping Roary on the go as much as possible, when she could keep him out of the bottle. It had been almost five years since Maxine had started working for Roary. Maxine had fallen for Roary from the very start, but Roary's grief had not allowed him to see it. Maxine's daughter, Chrissy, would sometimes come to work with her mom. Chrissy, now six years old, kind of looked at Roary as a father figure, a drunken father figure but a father figure nevertheless.

CHAPTER TWELVE

"GOOD MORNING, ROARY," the little girl said as Roary walked into the office at the Jacks Agency.

"Morning, Chrissy. How are you today?"

"Oh, I am fine. Thank you for asking. My babysitter is sick again, so I came to work with Mommy."

"Sorry, Roary. I didn't have another choice. Babysitter was sick, and my mom's out of town. She went up to Bakersfield to visit her sister."

"It's okay, Maxine."

"We got a job for you, Roary," Chrissy said with some authority. "It's a stakeout on a cheater. Mommy has all the details for you."

"How old are you again?"

"Six, Roary! I also help Mommy make coffee. Do you want some to take on the stakeout, Roary?"

"Yes, coffee sounds good. We have a case?"

"Yeah, one Jodi Dallis. Think her husband is cheating on her. Here is the address where he works. Her phone number, and she is paying cash."

"Cash, how much cash?"

"She had $300. We need the money, Roary, to pay some bills."

"Okay, Maxine, three days. That's it."

"Oh, don't worry, Roary, you will catch him. We know you will."

"Thanks, Chrissy. Anything else I need to know?"

The little girl stopped and thought about it. "No, but Daniel in my first-grade class, he kept pulling my hair. He'd better stop because my teacher, Ms. Brown, is going to make him stand in the corner if he doesn't stop, which is probably a good thing 'cause I might punch him."

Maxine handed Roary the folder with the information and a Styrofoam cup full of coffee. Then she fiddled with his tie a little and made a happy frown face as she nodded toward Chrissy.

"Thanks for the coffee, Chrissy, and good luck with that Daniel thing."

"Oh, it's all good, Roary. I have it under complete control."

"I am sure you do, Chrissy," and with that, Roary made his way out of the office and into the lobby of the hotel.

As Roary started out the front door, Bobby called him, "Hey, Roary, do you got a minute?"

"Sure, Bobby."

"What is going on?"

"Nothing much. Did you see Chrissy?"

"Yeah."

"You talking about the Daniel thing?" Roary said with a half grin.

"Yeah, she bent my ear pretty good this morning about it. Wouldn't want to be in his shoes," Bobby said, and they both laughed for few seconds. "Did you see the Metro blog in the paper, Roary?"

"No, I didn't."

"Well, here's the paper. Maybe you should read it for yourself."

"Okay, I will take it with me. Maxine got me a job on a cheater."

"You'll catch him, Roary. You always do."

Roary got in his 2004 Toyota Camry that he bought when he had wrecked his last car into the police cruiser four years earlier. Roary sat the coffee and the paper. Roary opened the folder inside the phone number to Jodie Dallis and a picture of her husband, Bart Dallis. Bart was a longshoreman at the Long Beach Harbor. He worked for a company called Hang Shipping Container. Roary made good time from North Hollywood down to the Long Beach Harbor. Roary parked in the parking lot across from Hang Shipping Container so he could get a good look at what was going on at the shipping port. Jodie Dallis's complaint read as her husband of three years had started coming home late and smelled of beer and perfume. Roary figured it was going to be a long day, but he still needed to identify Bart Dallis in person. Ten minutes till twelve, a catering truck showed up in the parking lot of Hang or as they're commonly called a roach coach. Roary went in for a closer look and bought himself some coffee and a doughnut. Roary had lost his tie and suit jacket. The ball cap, sunglasses, and windbreaker would be more suitable. He didn't have to look like a longshoreman, but he didn't have to look like a PI either.

Roary stood by the catering truck sipping his coffee and choking down a doughnut. Roary was beginning to think that Bart wasn't coming out for his break, but there he was, at the end of about thirty guys. He was big, 6'4" maybe, 250 pounds, with black shoulder-length hair and large bushy mustache. The name Black Bart would fit as a nickname. Roary finished his coffee as the men ordered their food and drink. He listened as they talked of the night before events and today's work, about their favorite football team getting its ass kicked on *Monday Night Football,* about the girlfriends being pissed off about having to watch football, or about a damn forklift that wasn't working quite right, mostly just things you would hear guys talking about.

Before Roary left to go back to his car, he heard Bart say, "We're going over to the Anchor Room after work for a beer or two." Roary thought, *I drove all the way down here when I could have just sat in my office and wrote down what this scenario was going to be. Longshoreman goes for beer after long day at work, cocktail waitress—young, perfumed— drinking beer and sitting on Bart's lap.*

But that wouldn't be doing his job. Besides, Roary was looking forward to testing the waters at the bar. Would he drink or not? Roary only had about three months on the wagon. Five o'clock came, and the workers started filing out of Hang Shipping Container. Some were headed home. Some were headed to their kid's ball game to try and catch the last few strikeouts to say "That's all right. You will do better next time." Bart Dallis was headed to the Anchor Room two blocks away for his last few drinks ever.

CHAPTER THIRTEEN

AT 5:30 P.M., Bart Dallis arrived at his favorite watering hole, a place where the thirty-two-year-old was known as a regular. Roary was only a few minutes behind Bart as he entered the bar. The Anchor Room was a lively bar with the capacity of about a hundred and twenty. It looked to be about half that right now. The bar was thirty feet long with twenty stools, fifteen tables for just drinking, four pool tables toward the back, and a ten-foot-long shuffleboard table along the wall leasing to the restroom. There were big screen TVs for watching sports throughout the bar. The place was just getting started for the night's entertainment. Roary found a table for two toward the middle of the room against the wall. This gave him a good view of the bar overall. Bart and his friends were three tables over closer to the pool tables.

A few hours went by and nothing out of the ordinary, just Bart having some beer and flirting with the waitress, one of the three young beauties working the floor, but so were half the guys in the place. Waitresses don't mind a little flirting. It's good for tips. All three of the waitresses seemed to know Bart. A hand on the small of the back and would lean in close when giving his order for more Budweiser and so far, all Roary had was a longshoreman trying to wind down after a long day on the docks. About 7:30 p.m., the place really got jumping as more longshoremen came in. Roary had switched from Diet Coke to near beer and back again. It was setting on his stomach very well. The fifty-three year old PI's kidneys weren't in that great shape either. So Roary made his way to the restroom to relieve himself. It was a relatively large restroom, clean as can be for a place like the Anchor Room. It had three urinals, two stalls, and three sinks. Roary was finishing up and washing his hands when he heard a strange laughter coming from one of the stalls. Roary wondered what could be so funny in the toilet. When Roary finished drying his hands, the laughter got louder, and it really crept Roary out. As Roary exited the restroom, he ran into Bart Dallis, face-to-face. Roary said excuse me and stepped to the side. Bart shuffled past and said, "Oh, you're all right, man," and went in the restroom.

Roary got a short twinge of guilt. Bart seemed like a big teddy bear, one even Roary wouldn't mind having a beer with, and Roary would really like to have a real drink right about now. Roary went back to his table and ordered another Diet Coke. He knew that Bart's night was not over yet, or at least that was what Roary thought. Five minutes later, all hell broke loose.

A guy came running out of the restroom, yelling, "Call the cops! There is a guy in there!" He was running so fast that he slipped and fell, hitting the floor pretty hard, but he was up in a flash and to the bar, yelling, "Call the cops and an ambulance!" Roary rushed to the restroom. As he opened the door, there was still dripping blood from parts of the ceiling. The walls were covered, along with urinals and stalls. Roary could see that the blood was still pumping out, which meant he was still alive. There was a huge pool of blood forming on the floor. Roary went to his side and knelt. Bart's eyes were glazing over. Roary didn't know if Bart knew he was there or not, but he hoped he did and that he was not alone. The pumping stopped. Both of Bart's ears were gone, and his throat was cut from ear to ear, very deep. Roary stayed with Bart till the police came. Nobody had seen anything out of the ordinary, but Roary had seen this work before. The last time put Roary in the bottle four years ago. Roary gave his statement and left quietly. Roary made his way back to his office in North Hollywood to clean the blood off and try and make sense of what happened.

When Roary arrived at the Beverly Towers, he parked his car where he always did, got out, and started into the building, when he heard it, a loud strange laughter coming from afar. It was the same laughter as earlier in the restroom. Roary immediately pulled his .38 snub-nosed revolver. Roary turned toward the laughter and yelled, "Who's there!"

The laughter almost sounded like crying, and then it was gone. Roary wanted to chase after the wailing laughter, but which way? The darkness was complete, and the sound had been far away. Roary stood his ground and yelled, "Come out where I can see you, you son of a bitch!" There was nothing but an old washed-up-cop-turned-PI covered in the blood of a longshoreman, whose wife Roary would have to talk to about her husband being killed by a murderer that followed him around, playing this deadly game.

Roary went on into the building to the office to clean up. He was tired. Roary managed a shower and to put on clean clothes. He retrieved a bottle of gin that was hidden in a file box in the office. Roary sat the bottle on his desk, thinking how much he really needed a drink. The day's events flashed like a neon light in Times Square. Brilliant shock waves biblically edited into his mind. Physically moved by his mind's eye with every blink of the monstrosity he had witnessed, Roary's hands were shaking. He knew that one drink would settle his nerves, but Roary had four months of sobriety, and somehow he had to be strong enough to hold on. Roary left the bottle of gin on his desk and sat on the sofa in his office. Sheer exhaustion quietly put his head down.

"What's this, Roary!" A loud, angry voice and bright sunlight through the office window brought Roary back to consciousness. It was Maxine holding the bottle of gin. "Four months, Roary! You couldn't even go a day on a simple cheating job without this crap!"

"Maxine, settle down!"

"No, Roary! Four years of you climbing in and out of a bottle of gin or vodka is long enough for anyone! And I am getting too old for it, Roary!"

"Maxine, I was just throwing it out. Just hadn't got that far yet."

"Well, I will take care of this one for you. What about the cheater?"

"His name was Bart," Roary said with a certain reverence in his voice. "Bart Dallis was killed last night at the Anchor Room lounge in Long Beach. His throat was cut ear to ear, and the ears were almost missing. And I am not positive, but I am sure he wasn't cheating, just a hardworking stiff that liked to have a few beers after a hard day's work, friendly enough guy that everybody seemed to like, including the three cocktail waitresses with the heavy-perfumed bodies bringing him his drinks."

"What happened, Roary?"

"I don't really know, Maxine. What I do know is my old ghost, the neckless murderer, is back." Roary paused for a moment. "May just be I am sober enough to notice. Whatever the cause, I don't feel that you or those around me are safe. Pretty sure he followed me back here last night."

"Did you call the police?"

"No, but I will go down to Metro today with what I do have. In the meantime, you need to go stay with your sister up in Bakersfield and take Chrissy with you. Just a few days till I know it's safe."

CHAPTER FOURTEEN

MAXINE AND CHRISSY left for Bakersfield to stay with Maxine's sister for a few days, while Roary tried to make sense of the last few days. The first place Roary would have to go would be Metro police headquarters to see the new chief of detectives, Greg Martin. The police blog that Bobby had been trying to get Roary to read the day before was about Greg's appointment to chief. That would not be good for Roary given their past. Roary had to go and see what new evidence, if any, the department had uncovered. At 10:40 a.m., Roary showed up at Metro to give his side of what happened last night at the Anchor Room. Frank Gonzales, second-grade detective, met Roary outside Chief Martin's office.

"Just make detective?" Roary asked.

"Yeah, about two months ago. The pay grade is a big help. You got history with the chief?"

"Yep, we got history."

"Have a seat, Mr. Jacks, I am just going to go over your statement from last night with a few more questions."

About that time, Roary heard an old familiar voice. "Hello, Roary." It was Capt. Greg Martin, the new chief of detectives and Roary's old partner.

"Hello, Greg."

"Why don't you come into my office, Roary?"

"Sure."

"You can follow up with Gonzales a little later."

"Okay," Roary said.

The two went into the office. "Nice digs, Greg. And congratulations on the promotion."

"Thanks, Roary. Seems like a long time coming. Now what has it been, four or five years?"

"Yeah, something like that, Greg."

"You know, Roary, we never found Kowarski's murderer or the murderer of the Lighthouse Hotel victims."

Those murders had put Roary off wagon for almost five years. And he was well aware of it.

"Anything new in last night's case at the Anchor Room?" Roary asked.

Martin's demeanor changed. "No! Not unless you have something to add, Jacks! Because it seems your old friend, the neckless murderer, is back. How long have you been sober, Roary?"

"About five months, and no, I haven't noticed anything out of the ordinary. Bart Dallis's wife was my client. She thought her husband was having an affair, which, as far as I could tell, he wasn't. One day, that's all I have to go on, Greg. I bumped into him, leaving the restroom five minutes before he was murdered. There was someone in the stall, laughing, when I was in the restroom, and then last night, when I returned to my office, there was someone with the same laugh in the dark. Couldn't tell where they were, but it was the same laugh."

"So you think this guy is playing some kind of game with you?"

"Yes, I think that's what he is doing," Roary said with an angry comeback.

"Well, you know the story, Roary. Let the police handle it."

"Let the police handle it! How many more people are going to die before the police handle it!" Roary barked.

"All right, settle down, Roary! It's been five years since the neckless murderer has been out and about."

"Well, that is putting it mildly," Roary said.

"The same time you were on your drunk."

"Yes, as far as I can tell, who knows, Greg, this guy could be committing murders all around me and I would not have known it? It seems he waits until I can recognize his work, waits until I am sober to commit the neckless murders. It is like he gets his jollies out of my torment over these murders."

"You may be right, Roary. I know it is a silly thing to ask you, Roary, but do you think you need police protection?"

"No, I don't think it would do any good. If he wanted to kill me, he would."

"Maybe it's a trap, Roary."

"No, this guy is way too smart for that. Besides, it would be dangerous. Somebody innocent could get hurt unintentionally."

"You're right, Roary. All I can say is be careful and let the police handle this."

"Sure, Chief!" Roary said with a sarcastic tone. "And if that is all, I will be going now."

"Oh, one more thing, Jacks."

"What is that, Chief?"

"Don't leave town. We may need to talk again."

"Sure. I'll be around." Roary made his way out of LA's finest to his car. There was one thing for sure: Roary would have to be more careful about his surroundings. He would have to start looking at everybody around him—sitting, standing, walking—like while he was in line at the store, double-checking mirrors or windows and storefront glass, and seeing if anybody was following him or, at times, just to be aware of everything that was going on around him. He would have to have a new way of thinking, a new way of looking at life—literally. He would start watching the small or slight nuances in everyday life, such as sounds that were out of place, odors that didn't smell right, or shadows looming behind him, leaving him aware, not paranoid but aware, ever aware. This was how Roary would catch the neckless murderer.

CHAPTER FIFTEEN

AFTER A FEW days, Maxine and Chrissy returned from Bakersfield. "How was your trip?" Roary greeted Maxine as she made her way into the office.

"Hot and noisy with all my sister's kids, but other than that, it was nice to see her."

"Where is Chrissy?"

"She is in school today, and I have to leave early to pick her up. How about you, Roary? Is everything all right?"

"Yes, still on the wagon. Oh yeah, I talked to Jodie Dallis and told her that I was pretty sure her husband was not cheating on her. And as far as I could tell from the police, he was just in the wrong place at the wrong time. She took that pretty hard. Maxine, I want you to keep a real close eye out on what is going on around here. If you see anything out of the ordinary, let me know, such as people lurking around or maybe following you or you see someone multiple times. Maybe hear something that doesn't fit with where you are or what you are doing."

"Okay, sure, Roary. Think someone maybe stalking us?"

"Just pay a little more attention to what is going on around you, but don't react to it if you do notice something. Just let me know about it, okay?"

"Should I be scared, Roary?"

"No. It just is better to err on the side of caution, okay?"

"Got it. Do you want some coffee?"

"No, I have already had two cups this morning. Maxine, I am glad you are back. It is time to get this agency back on its feet starting today."

For the next two years, the Jacks Agency worked its way back into the black. The agency took on jobs like missing persons and a lot of cheater cases. There were some petty larceny for a small company where the employees were stealing. All in all, the agency was making money. Roary integrated new technology into the company, such as high-speed Internet and smart phones, which instantly put him in contact with Maxine and the office information on the client. Roary also investigated in high-tech surveillance equipment, which included the latest in spy gear, camera watch, glasses that were two-way mirrors so you could watch what was going on behind you, and hyperbolic microphones good up to one block away. It could pinpoint a conversation in a crowded mall, and it looked like a regular ballpoint pen. Also included were night vision, stationary, motion-activated cameras with built-in mics small enough to fit into air vents at homes and companies. Sophisticated spyware were downloaded into company computers to monitor employees' day-to-day log-ins, which could be digitally recorded and reviewed or monitored in real time. Today's electronic thief could rob a company blind in a matter of minutes or do it slowly over a period of years. There was a lot of work to be done in today's investigation game, but Roary was getting older, and Maxine kept him informed and upgraded the best she could. She became the heart of the agency by putting jobs together that kept Roary moving. Things were looking up.

It had been two years since the last neckless murder had occurred, but Roary had started a rigorous vigilance of monitoring his environment, which included his car, apartment, and the office in Beverly Towers. But most of all, his personal space. Most people don't even notice their personal space. People walk in it, talk in it, and pass foreign objects through it all the time, such as perfume or germs, chemicals, sounds, light, or movement. They are so random and insignificant we just incorporate them into our daily lives. Roary Jacks, on the other hand, was acutely aware by that he studied everything in an orderly fashion, a routine, if you will. Some people call it OCD. Roary called it catch a killer.

CHAPTER SIXTEEN

ROARY MADE HIS way into the office about 10:00 a.m. It was a cool day in late October, but as usual, it was a gorgeous sunny morning.

"Morning, Maxine!"

"Good morning, Roary!"

Making his way into the second office, Roary sat at his desk. A moment or two later, Maxine came in with coffee and what looked like a file. "What do you got there?" Roary asked.

"Coffee and a new case for ya." She sat the coffee down on the desk in front of Roary. He immediately picked it and drank. Roary had a pretty good idea. The coffee was what got him into work every day. Maxine opened the file.

"You are going to like this one, Roary! A Mr. Steve Bowman, age forty-nine, Carson, California, aero engineer for Lockridge Space Technologies, says his ex-girlfriend is stalking him, keying his car, even left a dead rat on his doormat. He can't prove it, but he thinks she has been calling and hanging up on his phone about fifty times a day. He would like us to find out if that is what is going on. This is his phone number. He said to call him if you decide to take the case."

Roary took another sip of his coffee. "Okay, leave it on the desk, and I will give him a call. Maxine, can you see if Oliver is in his office?"

"Okay, in a few minutes!"

Later, Roary's intercom buzzed. "Yeah, Roary, Donna said he is in a meeting right now. Do you want her to call me when the meeting is over?"

"Yes, that will be fine." Roary finished off his coffee and studied the file.

"Oliver is on the phone, Roary," the intercom commanded.

"Okay, Maxine, I have it. Good morning, Oliver! How are you doing?"

"All right, Roary, what's up?"

"Lockridge Space Technologies, don't you know somebody over there?"

"No, not really, but I do own some of their stock."

"That's it. You told me you owned that stock."

"Why?" Oliver asked.

"A client I am thinking about taking on works there."

"Oh! What is his name?"

"Steve Bowman."

"Doesn't ring a bell, but Lockridge is big money for a little company. They are an industrial leader in aerospace communications. All of the big companies look to them for the latest and greatest advancements. That is why they are a great stock, a real moneymaker."

"Thanks for the insight, Oliver. How is everything else going?"

"Oh, pretty good, Roary. Why don't you and Maxine and the kid come out to the beach house on Saturday and make a day of it?"

"That sounds good, Oliver. Let me check with Maxine, and I'll have her let Donna know."

"Okay. Yeah, it will be like old times. Besides, can you keep a secret?"

"Sure. What's that, Oliver?"

"I am going to ask Donna to marry me."

"Oliver, that is great. Donna is a wonderful girl, and you are a very lucky man. Congratulations."

"Thanks, but I haven't asked her yet."

"Don't worry, Oliver, she loves the ground you walk on, and I will keep your secret."

"Thanks, Roary!"

"Okay, Oliver, I will talk to you later." Roary hung the phone up and hit the button on the intercom.

"Maxine, can you come in here for a minute?"

"Sure, Roary. I will be right in."

"Would you and Chrissy like to join me at Oliver's beach house on Saturday, maybe make a day of it?"

"Sure. We would love it at the beach, but this kind of sounds like a date, Roary."

"Yeah, I suppose it does. You need to let Donna know that we will be there about 11:00 a.m., if that is okay with you."

"That sounds great, Roary. Chrissy is going to love it, and I will call Donna right now and let her know."

"Okay, maybe I can pick you and Chrissy up about nine. We will grab a bite to eat on our way out. Is that all right?"

"Sounds great."

"Now I better get to work." Roary picked his smart phone and dialed Steve Bowman.

A deep voice answered the phone. "Hello!"

"Yes, is Steve Bowman there?"

"Speaking!"

"This is Roary Jacks of the Jacks Detective Agency. You called my secretary."

"Yes, it's about my old girlfriend. I think she may be stalking me."

"Yeah, I have your report here in front of me. Keying your car, phone calls but doesn't say anything, and a dead rat?"

"Correct. Yes, that is right."

"So do you want me to find out if this is her for sure?"

"Yes, that is it because I haven't caught her doing anything, but I know it is her. Look, I am pretty busy right now, but I will be off work at about 3:00 p.m. If you would like to meet me at my apartment in Carson, I will give you all the information on her that I have."

"Okay," Roary said.

"The address is 4400 Cherry Boulevard in Carson. The Cherry Bell apartments. Apartment number 62."

"Okay, Mr. Bowman, I will see you there. Four o'clock."

"Thank you, Mr. Jacks. Bye."

Carson was a good hour and a half from Beverly Towers, so Roary left around 2:00 p.m. to get there early. At 3:45 p.m., Roary circled the 4400 block of Cherry Boulevard, looking for a place to park. It was a good thing he had left early. Roary had to park about a block away and walk to the apartment complex, apartment 62. When Roary arrived and knocked on the door, it opened right away. It was quiet.

"Hello!" No answer. Roary stuck his head in and said, "Anybody home?" No answer. Roary pushed the door open. There didn't seem to be anyone about. Roary stepped through the doorway. "Anybody here?"

The next thing he recalled was his head feeling like it was splitting in half, finding the girl dead, being handcuffed, being taken to the hospital and then to police headquarters, and his old buddy Chief of Detectives Greg Martin chewing his ass about the neckless murderer again.

"Look, Greg, I told Detective Gonzales and some of your rookies everything I know. Maybe if I go to my office, I can tell you some more tomorrow, but right now, my head is splitting, and I just don't remember anything."

"All right, Roary, but first thing tomorrow, I want to know what you were doing there."

Roary took a taxi back to his office. There was no one at the lobby desk. Roary made his way into his office and turned on the lights. And there he was, sitting at Roary's desk in the dark. Roary hadn't seen him.

"Who are you? And what are you doing here?"

The man stood and pulled what looked like a Colt .45-caliber pistol from his coat. "Sit down, Roary!"

The way his head felt, it wasn't a bad idea. Roary sat in the chair across from his desk.

"It's time, Roary!"

"Time for what?"

"All these years, Roary, I am the one who hurt you. You still don't know after all these years."

"Know what?"

"You don't remember me, do you, Roary?" he said with slow drawl to his voice.

"How should I? Remember what?"

"All of it! All of them!"

"Them who? What are you talking about?"

"There it is. That is the emotion that lights up my life."

"What are you, some kind of nutjob?"

"Nutjob?" The man's eyes narrowed. "I would like to think of it as more godlike if you will!"

Roary began getting a sinking feeling in his gut. He recognized the man.

"Yes, Roary, it's me, First Lt. Steven Bowman, Naval Intelligence Service, Vietnam, 1975."

It came back to Roary like it was yesterday.

"Yes, that is right, Roary! Your first neckless murder, I recall. And I do recall every little detail of it. Most of all, the emotion and expressions that you displayed that day changed my life. The almost blinding light that came from you empowered me to rise above the earth. It was unbelievable. I had always gained power from the flesh, but your feelings released the power of the light. I was unstoppable as I am now. Roary, I have been there ever since. When you left Vietnam, so did I. When you were discharged from the Marine Corps, I resigned my commission in the navy and followed you out here to California. And almost every day and night, I have been with you for thirty-seven years. You've seen me. You've talked to me. I have touched you and whispered to you. I have been like your shadow. Sometimes just walking in its shadow allowed me to gain light from you. Roary, I have been face-to- face with you a hundred times. I have sat and ate my victim's ears and eyes at the table next to you. I have prepared many of your meals with parts of the sacrifice to me. They give me power. You give me light. God has given me absolute power with my sacrifice. Your light allows me to move above and be invisible. Your emotions are cracks in your soul. The expression releases the emotion, such as pain, sorrow, and anger. So you see, when you are lost and are in your finest misery, I am seen as a god. There have been times I thought I might light the world on fire with all of the power you have given me over the years."

THE FINAL CHAPTER

ROARY'S HEART WAS beating out of his chest. His eyes and ears were in disbelief. "How many?" Roary asked the madman.

"Why, all of them, of course!"

"The ones in Vietnam, here in the States, Oliver's second wife, Kitty!" Roary's anger overtook him.

"Easy, Roary," Bowman said as he held the gun on Roary.

"You want to know about Maxine and Chrissy, don't you?"

Roary froze in the chair. "Where are they, Bowman?"

"Safe right now! I just want you to know, Roary, how I have managed to rise to the level of a god. Thanks to you. Do you remember Kowarski, Roary?"

"Yes, police officer that was choked to death at police headquarters?"

"Yes, that's him. Do you know how I was able to just walk up and kill him? You see, I have applied many techniques over the years. Some are ancient Japanese shadow warriors able to paralyze their victims with a secret powder made of refined eucalyptus. It attacks the central nervous system to paralyze a person for up to ten seconds at a time. Just blow it into their faces, and they do whatever I want them to do. You don't really remember at all, do you?"

"No, I don't," Roary answered, barely realizing that he was saying anything. Roary's head was spinning, and gun or no gun, he was going to kill this son of a bitch. Bowman moved backward toward Roary's coat closet. He held the gun in his right hand, and with the left, he opened the door. There on the floor was Maxine and Chrissy. Their hands and feet were tied with what looked like tie wraps. Their mouths were bound with duct tape. As best as Roary could tell, they were still alive.

"So you see, Roary, as always, I command the control of life itself. Bobby Clark is also out there behind the desk in the lobby. You see, Roary, they are like my, well, should we say, subjects in my kingdom. They live, they die, with their only reason being my power source, my feast, my amusement, my lambs. But you, Roary, are something else."

"Why now, Bowman? After all these years and all of the killing, why tell me now?"

"Roary, it is time, time for me to make the leap, and I can only do that with all of your light, the ember which burns inside of you. I must have to make my leap into heaven's realm." Bowman slowly made his way back over to Roary's desk, leaving the closet door open.

Roary's mind was racing to the point he could not logically think of any option. To rush Bowman meant he would die, but he had to try. Roary jumped from the chair and flung it as hard as he could. The Colt .45 released a bullet, which struck Roary in the meaty part of his left shoulder. The momentum created by the impact spun Roary completely around 360 degrees. All Roary felt was a slight burning in his shoulder. Roary rushed Bowman with the chair full force on the bridge of the nose and bent holding it. With the gun still in his hand, just as Roary reached Bowman with a devastating right front kick to the face, another shot rang out. The bullet ripped through Roary's left side, and Roary temporarily lost consciousness while still standing.

As he opened his eyes, he saw Bowman falling face-first to the floor. The kick had found its mark. The nose cartilage had been driven into Bowman's brain. Roary lunged again, this time landing his full body weight on the back of Bowman's neck. A loud snap cracked through the air in the room. Roary rolled over to his back. Blood was spurting out of Roary's left side and shoulder. He would be unconscious soon from the loss of all the blood. Roary reached desperately for his cell phone to call 911. What seemed like forever he fumbled for it. He pulled the phone up close and tapped on the screen. There was so much blood it didn't want to work properly. Finally, 911.

"What is your emergency?"

"Beverly Towers, Hollywood, Jack Agency. I am shot. Hurry." Roary passed out, floating through space and light, muffled sounds from far off, the sound of time ticking. Roary was jolted to a room where people worked frantically in bright white light. Then Roary fell. He couldn't stop himself. He fell onto the people in the light. That was the last thing he remembered. The light hurt his eyes, and his mouth felt like as if he had swallowed a desert—Mojave or Sahara, one of those.

"Well, look who has come back from the dead." He recognized the voice, but his eyes still had not focused.

It was Maxine. "The doctors say you should make a full recovery, Roary! Can you hear me?"

Roary managed to nod. That was the way it went for the next couple of weeks, in and out of consciousness. At the end of a week, they were able to pull out the feeding tubes. Roary began to be cognizant of his surroundings and that Maxine had not left his side, that he was aware of.

"Water and close the blinds" were Roary's first words.

"Sure, honey. I will get right on it!" Maxine moved with a sense of thankful relief. "Here are some ice chips. That is all they say you can have. I'll get the doctor."

"No! Is he dead?"

"Yes," Maxine said in a somber voice. "Yes, you got that son of a bitch, Roary! You saved all of our lives—Chris, Bobby, and me."

"Good," Roary said. His voice was no more than a whisper.

"Okay, it is time for you to rest, Roary. You're going to need a lot of convalescing, and I am just the person to help you do it."

"Is he awake?" Greg Martin was standing in the doorway.

"Yeah, but he should really try to rest."

"That's all right. This will just take a minute, and I will do all the talking. The doctor said it was okay just for few minutes, if he was awake."

"It's okay, Maxine. Let him in."

"Roary, you sure are good at stopping bullets."

"Somebody's got to do it," Roary said with a grimace on his face.

"Well, we did a complete search of Steve Bowman's house out in Northridge and his office at Lockridge. That is how we figured out where he lived. There was quite a collection of the murders, each one categorized in detail, almost forty years of it. We don't know how many yet. We have to sort through it all—boxes of files, pictures, hundreds of pictures, trophies of kids, ears made into necklaces. The lab said he probably cured them in salt. Canned jars of eyeballs. We think he was eating them. And then there was a room of pictures of you and him, hundreds of them. Some were shot at a reverse angle. A lot of them are at murder scenes. It looks like you and he were great buddies for years. This was one sick son of a bitch. He had been stalking you for almost forty years. Well, get some rest, Roary. There will be an investigation, and we will need your cooperation."

"Sure, Greg."

"Okay, then get to feeling better, and I will see ya." The detective left the room. Soon after, Maxine reappeared.

"Okay, Roary, the doctor said he would be in a little later, so you need to try and rest to get your strength built up for the wedding."

"Wedding, what wedding?"

"You don't remember asking me to marry you?" Roary's mind began to race.

"Well, I . . ."

Maxine laughed aloud. "I was only kidding, Roary, but know it would be the smart thing to do once you are better."

"Yes, once I am better, it would be the smart thing to do."

The End

BUILT FOR YOU

ARTHUR C JETT

TABLE OF CONTENTS

CHAPTER 1

IF I COULD spell, would I write a book? If I wrote a book, would anyone read it? What would I even write a book about? Would it matter to anyone? Would it matter to me? Let's start a story about living in Ohio. That sounds like a place you might want to read about. A small town, yes. Somewhere by Michigan? Or how about Cincinnati? It's closer to Kentucky and Indiana as far as that goes, just normal people as far as people go. Nothing out of the ordinary, well, not on the surface anyways.

Jordan Williams was a cop-turned-private investigator because of a lack of moral compass. He'd been in trouble before for drinking and saying what was on his mind. Jordan had made mistakes, bad ones. Being drunk on the job and strong-arming thugs had gotten him fired from the Cincinnati police force in 2010. Yes, Jordan Williams was a lost soul. A need for money had pushed him to the dark side, where he drank so he did not have to see how bad he had gotten. Nevertheless, he suffered on as the world hadn't afforded him the courage to kill himself. He wasn't afraid because of pain; he just didn't have the courage to put an end to things.

Jordan had started a private investigation company. It was a shabby, rundown office on the riverfront. The office was filled with the smell of mold permeating the air from the water of the Ohio River that had risen too many times to lick the wood of the office building. It couldn't have been healthy to breathe in, though it didn't matter to Jordan. The cigarettes and whisky kept him from smelling the diseased floor and walls of his office. Cheap rye whisky was a mainstay of the thirty-five-year-old alcoholic. It had been a wonder that he even had a business at all. A lot of Jordan's work was delivering court orders to people behind on their rent or car payments. He even had the occasional husband or wife wanting him to track their spouse to see if they were being unfaithful. But Jordan William's life was about to change forever.

~

Jillian Campbell, a beautiful Cincinnati socialite, was the heir to a multi-conglomerate drug company. The twenty-nine-year-old slowly earned her family's respect as a businesswoman, with a natural ability to lead the company, the $140-billion-dollar company. Jillian had been groomed her whole life to run the Campbell empire, which had been created in the late '40s at the end of WWII by William G. Campbell. He was a chemist for the US Army and founder of the Campbell Drug Company, a brilliant chemist with no less than sixty patents. Jillian Campbell was no different as she held seven of her own patents, including the miracle drug Corasken. This drug could stop some forms of cancer in its tracks. Jillian's new endeavors consisted of cellular regeneration for post-cancer trauma. With a doctorate in internal medicine and a PHD in chemistry, her focus on cellular regeneration was premier in her line of work. Since the death of her father from lung cancer, she had dedicated her life to finding the cure.

~

Jordan Williams woke to the sounds of a work crew jackhammering the roadway across from the office where he had spent the night again because of blacking out on his third day of self-centered, alcohol-induced justice. The noise from the jackhammer did more damage to Jordan's head that felt just as severe as the blacktop being torn up outside at that moment. It was early, seven thirty in the morning, and the sun was brightly shining through the window of his office. A dusty gray hue erupted with a slight movement of his head from the office couch. Not knowing where he was after a night of binge drinking was standard. The piercing sounds of the jackhammer was making it hard to find a cigarette. He usually would make sure there was at least one cigarette for coming back to reality of his life. Even with the cigarette, which just added to the pounding in his head, he woke up unable to slip back to unconsciousness. Jordan was forced to face reality. The jackhammering continued as the cigarette smoke filled the room. His body and even his skin hurt. Halfway through the cigarette, his stealthy, cold blue eyes began to penetrate the room to find his favorite spot where his whisky bottle might be sitting, waiting for his company.

His eyes dashed left and then right, but he saw no bottle. Jordan groaned and then moved his head. "Damn," he said, "I'm going to have to get up."

After about ten minutes, he gave up on trying to find the bottle. He'd given up on trying to find any bottle for that matter. He told himself that today would be the day he would quit as he lit another cigarette, but that was the same old story he told himself for at least twenty years. He would start to clean up the dirty, ugly life that was Jordan Williams. No more covering immoral behavior or even maybe allowing it to flourish. The sad fact was that he had never been in control.

CHAPTER 2

THE CAR WAS racing out of control down Interstate 75. The riverfront exit was the last one before Kentucky. The sweet sixteen glossy black Cadillac sedan made the exit at 60 mph, sliding to a stop at River Road. Its tires spun as it hung a left-hand turn onto River Road. The car drove slowly past the small rundown business of River Road just blocks from the upscale corporate Cincinnati. The corporate side of Cincinnati was clean and beautiful, just where you wanted to be with its old and new architecture, Gothic and modern. Built by some of America's richest families, for centuries, the area was the hub of the trafficking of people, commodities, and ideals that have changed America and the world forever.

The Cadillac rumbled to a stop at 315 River Road, which was the address of that old Johanson freight building. Jordan William's office was located on the second floor of this building overlooking River Road. A large black man exited the car and entered the rundown first-floor entrance. As he approached the second-floor office, he began to pound on door number 3.

Jordan yelled in a highly annoyed tone, "Go away! The secretary is not here yet!" The pounding got louder. "Go away!" he screamed. "We aren't open today!"

In response to this, a deep baritone voice called out, "Open the door, Mr. Williams." Jordan began to think back on what bill he hadn't paid that would warrant this kind of collector. Jordan looked out the window and saw the Cadillac and knew that this was no bill collector.

Jordan went to the door and asked, "Who is it again?"

The same baritone voice rang out. "My name is unimportant, but my business will be very profitable for you, Mr. Williams." Jordan then opened the door and walked across the room as the big man entered the office and closed the door behind him. "Quaint digs," the man said as he looked about the shabby room and disheveled private investigator.

Jordan asked, "What do you want, big man?"

"As much as I can get, Mr. Williams. Have you heard of a Jillian Campbell?"

"You meant the one that everyone is thinking about changing Cincinnati's name to Campbell Jillian?"

"That's the one," said the pimp-looking big black presence in the room. "My name is Domino, and I want you to get ahold of a formula Dr. Campbell has been working on for years."

Even though his head was still pounding, Jordan began to laugh.

"You want me to present your proposal to her?" He laughed again.

"No, I want you to steal it. The formula is going to be worth billions, and your reputation precedes you. Your strong-arm techniques are legendary, and that's what we need to make her security understand we mean business."

"You must be crazy, Domino. First, there's an army of security in that building, and second, the Campbell Drug Company is worldwide. How could you possibly sell the formula?"

"Who said anything about selling it?"

Jordan's mind was already two steps into the plan to heist the formula. "What's in it for me?" Jordan asked as he moved behind his substantial Gothic desk that had come with the office space, along with two wooden chairs and a rough hide couch. This couch often also doubled as a bed. The big man reached under his fur-lined overcoat. Before he could get his hand clean of his coat, Jordan had his Glock 26 ten-round laser Accutane pistol pointing at Domino's head.

"Easy, Mr. Williams. This is just upfront money and some details you may or may not find interesting." Domino slowly pulled out a thick ten-by-twelve envelope and threw it on the desk. "Inside, you will find $10,000 in cash, including names and addresses of Campbell Drug Company employees. I need information, Mr. Williams—building locations, codes to those buildings, and as much access to the computer as I can get—so you can put down the gun and keep the ten grand. No questions asked. Or you can get a full share of a billion dollars. Think about it. My cell phone number is also in the package."

Domino lightly put his hands up halfway and backed out of the room. Jordan walked to the window and watched Domino enter his custom Cadillac and pull away. He then moved back to the envelope on the desk, opened it up, and pulled out the money first. It had been a long time since he had seen this kind of money. No questions asked. He then pulled out the list of names and began reading over them. There were foremen and heads of departments, such as development and research, as well as key names in security. That was just the start. If Jordan was to take the job, it would be done his way or no way. What Jordan really needed to know was where the bottle of rye whisky was. He lit another cigarette and decided to take a shower to clean up for the job at hand, putting together a plan for a billion-dollar heist. So that was simple. Today went from waking up from a three-day drinking binge, not having a reason to keep living, to pocketing $10,000 and a share of a billion-dollar heist. You could say things were looking up.

Domino pulled out on the northbound lane of I-75. As he did, his cell phone in the Cadillac rang. "Yeah?" he answered.

"Did he go for it?" the voice on the other end of the call asked.

"I don't know yet. He's supposed to call me."

"Well, make sure he does what he says. We need him for a bumbling distraction."

"Yeah, okay! I understand how this works!" Domino barked back at the voice.

"Calmly, Mr. Domino, calmly," the distinctively English voice responded. "You work for me, Domino, and termination is always a possibility. Keep me informed."

"Yes, I will," Domino said as the phone went silent. "Slimy bastard," Domino spoke under his breath as he maneuvered off the interstate.

Just north of Cincinnati in Lebanon, Ohio, half of a mile west of I-75, was the King Pin Gentleman's Club. This was where Domino made his headquarters for a very profitable sex and drug trafficking operation. It was also why Domino even knew about Jordan. He had robbed several of Domino's crack houses while Jordan was still a rookie cop. Jordan hadn't been a cop for at least seven years, but he was still well-known for his gutsy moves against drug lords. The words to describe his setups were smart and uncanny. Jordan used to go as far as pretending to be a chemist with the newest synthetic party drug. A lot of planning seemed to go into his elaborate schemes. If they didn't work, well, violence was a standard commodity. It was like your coffee in the morning. You could survive without it, but how much easier would life be with it?

Brute force was somewhat accepted in the Cincinnati police force at that time. Drugs and violence was running at an all-time high in the city. Something had to be done, and more often than not, a blind eye was turned on a successful officer's arrest methods when they had a high arrest rate for drug and violence offenders. Jordan Williams was the poster boy for this, but it wasn't long before rumors started circulating about missing evidence. Drugs or money started to go missing from evidence after each arrest, and after a series of complaints of police brutality, it was impossible for Jordan to remain one of Cincinnati's finest. To avoid prosecution, the corrupt cop resigned, and that was fine for the criminal side of Cincinnati. Not so much for Jordan, though, who was fast-tracking his way into a bottle. Domino hadn't forgotten, and now Jordan would be the fall guy for the biggest heist ever.

CHAPTER 3

JORDAN DECIDED TO clean himself up. He knew he needed to make a trip to the Campbell Drug Company to look for himself. The complex alone was spread out over six city blocks, and that alone was intimidating. Jordan stepped from the shower, dried off, and started to get dressed. He began to have this odd feeling that someone was watching, though, so he looked around the small four-room office. He couldn't see anything, but his hair was still standing on end. Jordan moved slowly, first to his desk to retrieve his Glock 9 mm, because whoever was here would get the full issue. He then moved back to the kitchenette and then the small restroom. Nothing. He thought that maybe it was a case of the delirium tremors. He had been on a serious drinking binge for at least three days. The presence remained focused on Jordan. He finally finished getting dressed, gathered his car keys, locked his office, and stood there for a few moments observing the space in the hall. He just couldn't shake the feeling that he wasn't alone. Down he went to the underground garage, and he made his way to his car. Twice he stopped and put his hand on his gun. "Whoever is there, come out, or I will shoot you!" No one came.

Jordan pulled his car onto River Road East toward I-75 North. As he drove north, Jordan came to a realization. *At 8:29 a.m. on I-75? What the hell?* The Campbell building was off exit 7, but somehow he had driven twenty-two miles past that exit. What was more disturbing was that he didn't remember driving that far at all. His mind was racing. Was it a blackout from his drinking? Some kind of stroke? Epilepsy maybe? Whatever it was, he was visibly shaken from it. What he didn't know was that whatever it was wasn't going anywhere. Whatever it was was already inside him.

Jillian Campbell entered her twenty-third-floor office at Campbell Drug Company in Downtown Cincinnati. She was greeted by her secretary,

Mary Ann Miller. She had been the secretary of Jillian's father for many years, and now she was Jillian's friend, confidant, and private secretary.

"The reports on stem cell growth from microgravity are on your desk. NASA sent them early this morning."

"Oh, that's great!" Jillian exclaimed.

"I thought you would like that," Mary Ann said. Jillian walked into her office to lay down her things and picked the report. She began to read, and about the same time, Mary Ann entered her office with a tray of coffee. "Here you go, dear," she said as she began to pour Jillian a cup. "Would you like me to schedule a video conference with David Hargate in the lab?"

"Yes, and also Jerry Blackwell in legal. Let's make it for ten thirty this morning. Thank you, Mary Ann." Jillian began to read the NASA report again. She was looking to see what the results were on her experiment, regenerating in zero gravity. She was trying to accelerate cellular growth by not having the pressures of gravity in a controlled environment. The results looked very promising. Just to have the genes survive the trip was exhilarating. "Yes!" Jillian said out loud, giving herself a small fist pump. Her calculations had been better than expected. Jillian's experiment had consisted mainly of ruptured genes and membranes fused in a hyper-oxygenated solution. She had no idea that her life was about to change forever.

~

The mold grew rampant along the riverfront. The sidewalks, buildings, and bridges—depending on the time of year, it was everywhere. Jordan had noticed the smell as he exited his car in the parking garage. It was stifling, and he grabbed for his sinuses between his eyes. "Wow, that smell is strong today," he muttered to himself. His trip to the Campbell Drug Company had been a bust. He remembered nothing of the trip, and it was already 4:00 p.m. Jordan thought, *A drink or two should bring things back into tune.* He couldn't think straight. He felt as if he were shifting through time instead of being present in the moment. His Jack Daniels only had one-third of it left. He quickly poured two fingers into a dirty glass. It went down in one gulp. "Hell yes," he said as he quickly poured another shot with the same result. The whisky was starting to do it. Jordan was beginning to get some focus and steely gray companionship that the booze afforded him, a partner to protect him from the world, a friend to blur out all the harsh realities life threw at him. Who needed real friends when you had a friend like Jack? In truth, it was the only way for Jordan to survive the monster within as his moral compass wobbled wildly out of sync with his reality. The Campbell job would need a lot of planning and a lot more of Jack Daniels. He would try again later today, but right now, his Russian friend, Smirnoff, had to be located. A good spot to look would be Joey's Liquor Store. He would definitely help with the plans.

Snap! Another shift in time and space and Jordan was now entering his room again without a single memory of where he had been. Two bottles suggested Joey's, but he had no idea. He would have to check the clock and find out what time, or day, it was. If Jordan did not have the plans soon, Domino and company would terminate Jordan's life contract. The sunset and ember glow shone through the window of Jordan's office. It would be dark soon. The city of Cincinnati, or at least its underbelly, would be coming alive soon. The smell of the Ohio River was tolerable. Even the thick dirt smell of the mold was subdued. As he started on the second bottle of vodka, a bright light began to flash green, blue, and purple, like lasers piercing through his skull. At first, the pain was excruciating, but then it changed. Jordan began to levitate and hover five feet off the ground. In his mind, Jordan was still lucid. He began to reel with unbridled pleasure, conscious of the moment, hallucination and delirium tremors encroaching on their pinnacle, likely due to alcohol poisoning. Or at least that was what he thought in that moment. Signs and symbols, an icon? A message from beyond perhaps. Then Jordan was aware. He understood that he was between time and space, and he was stone-cold sober. The ease of control and the understanding of his being was calming and exhilarating in parallel. Being aware was empowering.

He was now able to move to different spots in the room simply by thinking about being there. What other powers had he acquired? He wondered if he could time travel. Simply by thinking about shifting through time and space, the light in the room would darken and become light again with his motion through time. He went from late afternoon back to the bright morning light in a flash of a second. He could hear sound in coded bits. Audible digits, when unscrambled, became noises and conversations from afar. It seemed that it was as far away as half a mile. He could hear the music at a bus stop coming from a young man's iPhone. All those audible digits became sounds he could understand and decipher. He could also see into the room next to him and two doors down. Not only could he see the people in that room, but he could also see the water in the pipes as well as the gas undulating with a light blue iridescence. Jordan understood the compound that it took to make up the gas and the water on a molecular level.

Laser lights flashed again and again in blue, red, and green hues throughout the room. Jordan was no longer afraid. He was simply surprised and filled with glorious surrender to the experience, to what he had become and gained. He was totally self-aware. Jordan Williams had become a different being. The office phone rang, and everything that was occurring ceased to exist as quickly and suddenly as it had appeared. It was suddenly quiet and dim again sans the ringing of the phone. Jordan reached for the phone, hesitant as he was still unsure of what had just occurred. He had a lot of questions, all of which needed answering, but the most persistent was the hello on the other end of the phone.

"Hello? Jordan, is that you?" the voice asked again.

"Yes," he answered hesitantly, "this is he."

"This is Domino. We need to meet. It's been a week, and I need to know your plans on the Campbell deal."

"Okay, but let's not talk on the phone," Jordan said. "It's not safe. Meet me at River Down's Racetrack at three o'clock in the handicap section, number 14. I'll be there, Domino," Jordan said as he hung the phone up.

The track was wet today, but the horses were running just fine. A light mist fell across the track on its participants. Jordan and Domino met on the top row of the bleachers. Domino spoke first. "What do you have for me? What is the plan?"

Jordan just sat there with a glazed look in his eyes, staring out over the track. "I have something very special for you and the whole world."

Domino looked at him, even more perplexed than before. "Come on, quit screwing around," he blurted out, even more annoyed than before.

Jordan's stare adjusted as Domino's words became louder. "Dr. Campbell's formula will be in our control soon, and that's all you need to know."

"No! You are wrong! I need to know what your plans are!" Domino bellowed out, this time with a much sterner tone.

Jordan turned his head slowly in the direction of Domino, and as he did, he froze time. He stood and began to circle around Domino, who was also frozen. Jordan got real close to Domino as he looked into the eyes of the big man. "I want to know it all, Domino. I want to know who you are working for and what the real deal is with this heist." Without saying another word, Jordan was able to hook into Domino's brain and see his thought process. And just like that, he knew Domino's emotions and the inner workings of his brain. He could sense the blood moving around through Domino's veins. He could feel the life sparks that fired in Domino's brain. Jordan Williams could see it all. But who is the English boss, the man running the show? "What's his name, Domino?" Jordan forced his will upon the big man.

"I don't know, but he is high up in the world syndicate. He's only contacted me by cell phone so far. He's just using you for a distraction, a cover-up of what is really going on. We needed a patsy, and you're it." Even though Domino was frozen in place, Jordan could hear Domino chuckling in his head. Jordan used his willpower and applied great force to the inside of Domino's skull, causing tremendous pain; however, Domino remained motionless.

"It's not so funny now, is it, big man? I won't kill you this time, but you are going to give me the Cadillac in the parking lot."

"okay!" Domino screamed in his mind, clearly still in distress. "Whatever you want!" Jordan slowly began to release his grip on Domino's mind, and as he did, Domino's body began to collapse. He shuddered and encased his head with his arms as if to protect it from any intrusion again.

"The keys, please," Jordan said. Shaking—in fear or pain, Jordan was unsure—Domino retrieved the keys from his pocket and handed them over. "You're getting off easy this time. Do you understand me?" Domino slowly, gingerly, shook his head. Jordan could sense it now. The fear emanating from Domino was stifling. It almost seemed as if he were suffocating simply from fright. Jordan walked to the Cadillac and away from Domino, murmuring, "Nice ride." Jordan started up the custom car, moving it onto the highway all the while thinking that it was about time to meet Ms. Campbell.

The private eye parked the sweet sixteen Cadillac in the visitors' parking lot at the Campbell Corporate Headquarters. He walked into the lobby, straight to security, and tapped into their minds. Once he made a connection, he planted the thought that Jordan had an appointment with Dr. Campbell. They pointed toward the elevator and unanimously said, "First elevator, twenty-third floor." He entered the outer office, where he was met by Jillian's secretary, Mary Ann Miller.

"Do you have an appointment, sir?"

With a glance, Jordan said, "Why, yes, I do." As Mary Ann reached for the phone to page back to Jillian, Jordan held up his hand and abruptly said, "Don't bother. She's expecting me."

"Oh okay," Mary Ann said compliantly. Jordan let himself into the big office. It was well styled, and you could tell she didn't spend most of her time here. She likely spent most of her time in the Campbell Laboratories.

"May I help you?" Jillian asked. She was surprised. Mary Ann never just let someone walk in. She looked past Jordan to the outer office for Mary Ann.

"No, Dr. Campbell, I am here to help you. I don't know why, but I have a need to help you. My name is Jordan Williams, and I am going to put you at ease by giving you a key code to the formula you have been working on." He handed her a piece of paper as he said all this.

"Look, Mr. Williams, I don't know who you are or how you got in here, but I am going to find out," she said with a stern tone. At the same time, she looked over the piece of paper Jordan had given her. Jillian was astonished. "Where did you get my formula?" He said nothing and continued to walk around the room, examining everything as if he were stripping it down to the studs in his mind, which he was, in his head. Jillian fell quiet as she studied the formula. Her deep eyes began to read in disbelief as not only was her formula correct, but also the solution was homogenously composed and her revolutionary mixture on paper actually worked. Her next question that broke her silence was "Who did this formula? Mr. Williams, is it?"

"Yes, of course, I did the formula, and please call me Jordan."

"Okay, Jordan, how did you come up with these answers?" She held up the paper with the formula on it.

Jordan smiled and said, "You might want to sit down for this next part." Jordan stopped his pacing and began, "I retrieved the formula from your mind. I then broke down the elements and compounds and quantitatively measured them. I then systematically discharged them until the correct answer was identified."

"You must be kidding," Jillian said in disbelief. "You retrieved it from my mind and solved it? Where is your laboratory?"

"I do not have a laboratory. I simply did all the calculations in my head. That particular formula took about two minutes to complete."

Jillian laughed. "Two minutes? I have been working on this for two years, and you say you managed to figure it out in two minutes without a laboratory?"

"Yes." Jordan reached into his pocket and pulled out another piece of paper and handed it to Jillian. "I believe this was another formula of yours."

She examined it. "Why, yes, it is a part of a formula I just received from NASA. But how . . ." and before she could finish her thought, Jordan was inside her head.

"Can you feel me, Jillian? Do you understand me?"

"Yes, I do."

"Don't be frightened. I will not hurt you." He moved her body from behind the desk and out and around to the front of the desk. In front of Jillian, there were screens of formulas being calculated. "This is how I came up with the answers to your questions." She watched as screen after screen appeared and disappeared in her mind. Then suddenly, it was all gone. She was standing in front of Jordan, who was no longer in control of her mind or body. "So now that you believe me, I can get on with protecting you. There are evils in this world who want to harm you. Up until yesterday, I was one of those evils. That was until my newfound powers kicked in, and now it seems I am a very changed man . . . Lucky for you."

"Powers?" Jillian asked in a very skeptical voice.

"Yes, Ms. Campbell, I know it is hard to believe that I have powers. But believe this, it is not safe for you here, and we should leave now."

"I have no intention of going anywhere with you, Mr. Williams!"

"Please call me Jordan. If I may, I will call you Jillian. Is that all right with you?" He began looking around the room again, and then he tapped into her mind. "I am only trying to help you." She did not know why, but she didn't feel threatened. If anything, she felt safe and content, peaceful and at ease. "They are coming. We have to leave now."

As Jordan said this, Jillian's office door flew open. Four military-dressed assailants entered the room with weapons drawn. Jordan stepped in front of Jillian. One of the men shouted for him to move out of the way, or they would kill him, but it was too late. Jordan was already in their minds. The men turned their weapons on one another and began to fire at one another's feet and legs. The small burst of carnage left room for Jordan and Jillian to make an escape. "We have to go now!" Jordan shouted as he grabbed her arm and dragged her out of the office. Jillian looked around the outer office, but her secretary was nowhere in sight.

"Where is Mary Ann?" she asked worriedly.

"She is not here. I'll explain later," Jordan said as bullets began to fly by their heads. Two more gunmen were crouching by the elevators. Jordan yelled, "Hang on!" and, with that, began to slow time. Jillian felt weak at the knees. Everything was now moving very slowly. She watched as she moved her head and watched a bullet pass by at a snail's pace. Jordan looked at her and said, "I know, right!"

"Is this real?" she muttered.

"Yep, you're dodging bullets! Pretty cool, huh!" He smiled, and as they went into the elevator, Jordan pushed the lobby button. The elevator began to descend in real time, and as it did, they could hear the gunshots ringing outside. The elevator remained quiet until Jillian spoke.

"Those men are after my formulas."

"Those men are just crooks, world-connected crooks, but still just crooks."

"Okay, well . . . what about your powers? Where did they come from?"

"I honestly don't know where they came from. More and more manifest themselves as the days pass."

"What do you mean 'more and more'?"

"Well, I guess we have a minute. Let me explain. First of all, I can levitate things, including myself."

"Fly . . . You can fly?" Jillian asked.

"No, I believe I said levitate. And somehow I know what things are at a molecular level just by looking into them."

"Can you see what's inside these walls?" Jillian asked as she placed a hand on the walls of the elevator.

"Yes, not only can I see what is inside but I can see what the density is and the structure compounds and the resistance. The screen I showed you in your head was merely a tracking board. If I want to know how something is made or what it is, I pull it on a board, and it will tell me. Imagine like this, an entire room will become a teaching cube with all of the formulas running at once, and that is how I control time and movement. Get this, I don't think my abilities are from this earth!"

"So you are saying that something from outer space is controlling you or is just giving you these powers?"

"Yes, I think that's it exactly," Jordan said. As the doors to the elevator began to open again, he said, "Time's up!" He began to slow down time again as six men with automatic weapons lifted their weapons and began to shoot from their stations around the parking garage. Jordan fired three shots from his 9 mm. His bullets zoomed toward their targets in real time to find their marks. Jordan grabbed Jillian's arm and gave her a slight push away from him. "Stand here," he said. The M249 light machine gun on one of the men rang out multiple shots. It only took Jordan a moment to realign the shot trajectory, and then the guns fell silent. Time sped back up to reality again, and Jillian could hear the last gasp from the men as the realigned bullets found their marks. "Come on, let's go," Jordan said as he took her by her hand.

She resisted. "No! You just killed those men!"

"It was them or us! They were firing before the doors even opened!" He tried to drag her away again, but again, she resisted. He sighed. "Fine. If it makes you feel any better, I will only wound them from now on, but for now, we have to go." Jordan pulled her to the passenger door of the sweet sixteen Cadillac, forcing her in ever so gently. She fit in the seat like fine Italian gloves. Jordan got in and started the car. He could see how scared she was, but he could also see how extraordinarily beautiful she was.

"Where are we going?" Jillian asked.

"Somewhere safe. You will need some sleep soon, Jillian."

"I will need sleep soon, yes, but what about you?"

"I don't know if I will ever sleep again. Those visions tend to come up as they please. Sometimes I am in and out, but I think I have a handle on it."

"Do you really think it's aliens that have taken you over?"

"That's the best I can come up with right now. These powers just feel bigger than anything that could possibly be from Earth." Sometime later, they pulled down a wooded road about two hours outside Cincinnati.

"What is this place?"

"This is an old cabin on the Ohio River. It belonged to my greataunt, and it's a good place to lie low for a day. I have to return my associate's car. You will be safe here. I won't be gone long." The car quickly came to a stop in front of a rundown cabin. Jillian could hear the water from the river in the darkening distance rolling calmly. She thought about how relaxed all the sounds made her feel. Jordan forced the old pine door open, and as he did, the smell of musk and dust hit the pair in the face. "Careful," Jordan started to say as he entered the old cabin. "It's been a few years since I've been here." He made his way toward the center of the room, where he knew the table was. He felt around for a few seconds and found an old storm lantern. He shook it and said, "Good, there is still fuel in it." He made his way to the fireplace mantel and retrieved a box of matches. He lit the lamp, and the light from it illuminated the very rundown but somewhat cozy two-room, early-turn-of-the-nineteenth-century cabin. It had a river rock fireplace, a potbellied stove, a sink along one wall, a comfortable larger high-back chair, and a table with two chairs.

"It feels like a good place," Jillian said.

"My aunt Clara loved it. I remember loving coming here as a kid. Hmm, she was such a good person. Never heard a bad word come out of her mouth. Those were some of the best times of my life."

"Kinda like Mary Ann, my secretary!"

"Yes," Jordan said. "She was also your father's assistant. Yes, she is the key."

"The key to what?" Jillian asked.

"Us, of course! I remember her from when I was a child."

"That's impossible!" Jillian exclaimed.

"We just need to put the pieces together. Don't you see that this isn't a coincidence that you and I are here? Jillian, I am pretty sure I am here to protect you. I don't know why or how, but I am going to find out."

"You are out of your mind."

In that moment, he let himself into her mind, and he was in her head. "Yeah, now I am in your head." He was in the twilights of her mind, and then he released her mind and body and began to walk to the door. "I have to return my friend's car. Stay here. Do not leave this cabin. I will be back in two hours."

"Jordan, I am not staying here by myself. I am coming with you."

"No! Just wait here. It's too dangerous."

"I am coming, and you can't stop me." At that moment, Jordan used his levitation powers on the wingback chair and lifted it a foot in the air. He dropped it to try and prove a point. He then looked into her eyes and regretted it. Her eyes were so blue. He knew the sky must get jealous as she watched birds fly and clouds part. It was as if the heavens left two drops of the sky in her eyes. Again, her beauty captured his heart and mind as he slowed time. Jordan could not mark his inner feelings. Walking slowly toward her, he thought that she was a Venus de Milo sculptured goddess for him alone. Jordan lightly brushed the gold-spun velvet strands of hair back from her face, lightly touching her cheek as he did so. In that moment, all the corruption in his life, all the bad things he had done, left his soul. Jordan Williams knew that she was his reason for living and his purpose in life. All that came before her was just a waste of time. In that moment, Jordan fell in love, heart and soul. A hundred thoughts ran through his head, but the most prevalent question was how to save her. Jordan then released time and stepped away from Jillian.

"All right, you can come, but you have to do what I say if you want to get through this, if we are going to get through this." The two left the cabin, and at that moment, something stirred in Jillian's soul. It seemed as if Jordan had stirred it. She thought that he was quite rough around the edges, but he was handsome and safe. He was definitely a take-charge type of guy. Maybe that was why she found that she was attracted to him. Whatever it was, she was not afraid. Right now, her life was in his hands, and she wouldn't have it any other way.

CHAPTER 4

DOMINO SAT IN his office at the gentleman's club, afraid because he knew Jordan would be back. He loaded his 355 Magnum and drank a shot of whisky to try and calm his rattled brain from the thoughts of Jordan having control over it. The sweet sixteen Cadillac rumbled westward toward Cincinnati.

Jordan's first priority was to level the playing field, and that meant stopping the crime syndicate, cut the head off. He parked outside the gentleman's club. "All right, Domino, come out to get your car!" Jordan shouted at the building, knowing Domino could hear him. Domino stood and put his gun in his coat and began to walk outside to his waiting car. Jordan was waiting with the window rolled down. "How's the head, Domino?"

"Okay," he answered with a zombie stare. Jordan peeped into Domino's mind.

"Where are the boss's offices?"

As Jordan began to apply some pressure to Domino's mind again, Domino cried out, "Little Whipper's downtown, the old Kaiser building, top floor!"

"How many men are waiting there?"

"Maybe twenty or more. Since you have been killing everyone, they have people on every floor, expecting you to show up."

"That's a good fellow," Jordan said. "Don't cross me ever again, Domino. If anyone tries anything against me or Ms. Campbell ever again, you'll take care of it. Got it?"

"Yes, Mr. Williams, I understand perfectly."

"Good. Now give me the gun you've been hiding under your coat." Jillian was relieved that Jordan had not killed the man. Maybe there was hope for Jordan after all. Jordan looked at Jillian and said, "Next stop, the

Kaiser building, but first, I need to see how far this mind control works." Jordan pulled the car up the road some short ways from the gentleman's club. "Can you see the front door, Jillian?"

"Yes, I can." With his back to the front door, Jordan used his mind to make Domino run in and out of it three times.

"How many times did Domino come out of the building?"

"Three times," Jillian replied.

"Okay, perfect. Now we know that my mind control works at least one-fourth of a mile from my target. When we get close to the Kaiser building, I am going to need you to stay in the car so we can make a fast getaway."

"Okay," Jillian said.

The Cadillac pulled up to the curb half a block from the Kaiser building in Downtown Cincinnati. The building had been headquarters for a large automaker in the early '30s and then an insurance company in the '40s and '50s until it was bought by a large multi-conglomerate based out of London, England, in 1962. It became a foothold for a secret crime syndicate known as the Common. They were into every scheme imaginable such as money laundering, murder for hire, robbery, drug trafficking, extortion, and racketeering. Now they were looking toward a new project, illegal drug trade. Pharmaceuticals was a big business. They had done their homework, and it had shown the Campbell Drug Company brought in big profits, well beyond their expectations. This made Jillian Campbell the perfect target for the Commons. Jillian's father had been aware of such forces of evil in the world, which was why her father had altered Jordan's DNA before he was born, to protect the Campbell family, to protect Jillian Campbell.

The time-released genes in Jordan's DNA were timed out and as precise as a Swiss-made watch. Yes, Dr. Campbell Sr. was a genius, a voyeur of the future. His formulas were almost godlike, and his work on human genome research was light-years ahead of its time. He studied human modification, and Jordan was one of the babies whom Dr. Campbell performed secret tests on. Jordan's whole life began in a test tube. The chemically and mechanically engineered fetus was created with a purpose to every cell. Every cluster of cells was engineered to release at a certain time, and all those clusters of cells grew to create Jordan and the man he was today. He was created to have perfect skill set to protect Jillian Campbell, and all the cells were timed to release to the perfect millisecond.

Where was the secretary? Where was Mary Ann? The doctor's confidant, the overseer of the Campbell empire, was nowhere in sight when Jillian was attacked at the office. Jordan tapped the picture in his pocket, the picture he had retrieved from the cabin, a picture of his aunt Clara. The two drove on in silence. The Cadillac slowed and then stopped across from the Kaiser building.

"Look, Jillian, I need you to stay here while I check on our friends inside. When I give you the signal, bring the car to the front entrance of the building," Jordan said in a matter-of-fact voice. "I won't be long."

"What is the signal?"

"I will flash the lights on the car using my mind, twice."

"Yeah sure, I got it, Jordan. No killing . . . right?" she asked in a soft and concerned voice. Jordan looked at her and cracked a small smile in the corner of his mouth. He then turned and walked toward the back entrance to the building. Jordan began getting signals from the building. It seemed like plans, compounds, water and electrical diagrams, and blueprints. The door was locked but only for a moment as he quickly dissected and kinetically moved the tumblers around in the lock. He finally heard a *click*, and he was in. Once inside, Jordan mapped out the route to the penthouse, but something didn't feel right. Some of the floors were dark, appearing like black stripes in the building blocks that was the Kaiser building. It seemed like a large puzzle, so Jordan's mind began putting it together one piece at a time. Movements on the other floors suggested thirty or more live bodies. He would have to work fast and did not know how long his endurance would last.

On the first floor, two security guards approached. As best as he could tell, they were legitimate hardworking stiffs, but they needed to be incapacitated while he worked. A restroom was directly on the right of him that would do just fine. Jordan immediately froze them in their steps. "Okay, into the head for you two." As they entered the restroom, they fell onto the floor, incapacitated. The extra squeeze on their minds afforded him this opportunity. On the second floor and then the third, and so it went until the fifth floor when hot bodies began to show in his mind. These bodies were heavily armed because of the composite makeup. Six figures were lying in wait for their prey. *Not today, soldiers of death,* Jordan thought as he systematically taunted out a few of the men at a time. Two of the black-clad men came out together and opened fire. Jordan rolled to avoid the shots and managed to shoot as well, but his bullets found their marks in the upper torsos of the men. They were down but not dead, just as he had promised Jillian. The other men attacked, guns ablaze. Jordan slowed time and calmly walked through the hall past the gunfire. Jordan relieved them of their weapons and handcuffed them all together around a large water pipe in the hallway. He also relieved them of their pepper spray, thinking it might come in handy later. On up through the floors he continued. In floors 7 and 8, he used the pepper spray, the burning, stringing, blistering pepper spray, to neutralize his would-be assailants. By slowing time, he could easily walk up to them and spray. The more he used his powers, though, the more he felt something was very wrong. He was profusely sweating; his head and his arms were turning bright red as if he were overheating. Yes, that was it; he was overheating. It was like an old car trying to go up a steep hill. Jordan pressed on, though, up through to the ninth and tenth floors to the penthouse. It was completely dark, his superior senses evading him as he felt like his blood was boiling.

"Yes, Jordan," a feminine voice rang out of the dark shadows.

"Who's there?" Jordan demanded to know with a loud, commanding voice.

"Oh, Jordan, you break my heart! You don't know the voice of your old aunt Clara?" A chilling fit of laughter followed. "It's me, Jordan, Aunt Clara." Jordan's mind raced. The voice he heard was exactly that of his aunt Clara, but that was impossible. The voice spoke again, "It has been a long, long time, my boy, but here we are again. I have followed your life, I expected more, but I suppose the results are all the same. You and I and Jillian, all together again. Are you feeling uncomfortably warm? Yes, I should think you are. Oh, say hello to Jordan, will you, Jillian?"

"Hello, Jordan," a voice out of the dark said. It was Jillian, but how? He had left her in the car. They must have grabbed her while he was making his way through the building, at least that was what his rushing mind was telling him. Jordan's body temperature was rising at an alarming rate, sweat began dripping from his forehead.

"Kinda hot in here, don't you think, Aunt Clara?" Jordan asked.

"No, not at all, Jordan. The heat you are feeling is being generated by nanobots, micro biomechanical bots. You had somewhere close to three hundred, but now they are probably totaling close to three million throughout your physical makeup. You see, Jordan, your nanobots were a special breed. They build and compute and reproduce by the millions, getting smarter and stronger and more complex. All of which are now controlled by me. You do see, Jordan, don't you? A high-volume digital frequency controls your nanobots, and I have the controllers to the nanobots in you and now in Jillian," said the voice as Mary Ann Miller stepped from the shadows.

"Yes, Jordan, I am your aunt Clara. I am also the deep voice with the English accent that Domino would take orders from on the phone. So as you know by now, I control a large part of the world, both legal and illegal, and you two are not the only 'bot babies' I have. Granted, you two are the most advanced of your kind. I have spent most of my life building and nurturing you both. You are my family."

"I don't feel like family very much right now, Aunt Clara," Jordan said.

"Oh, Jordan, my boy, this is business, the reason you were made in the first place. Here's the deal, Jillian is smart, very smart, just like her father. She and her nanobots create. She is quite literally a genius. You, on the other hand, are a warrior bred to protect Jillian and myself and whoever I program you to protect."

"Whether I want to or not?" Jordan asked.

"Yes, that is right, Jordan, whether you want to or not. I control what you feel or think at my leisure."

"But you cannot tell what I am thinking," Jordan said.

"No, but I can take control at any time." Jordan felt the heat of his body rising higher.

Finally, Jillian spoke, "Jordan, she is losing control over you. That is why your bio bots are overheating. Keep fighting her. It's time we are free," she pleaded.

Mary Ann Miller waved her left hand over her right arm, and a six-inch screen appeared above it. She pushed a few numbers in on the screen, and Jillian was no longer able to speak or move. She pushed a few more numbers, and Jordan's vision started to go dark he couldn't see or hear, but he was ready. More of Aunt Clara's henchmen came out of the dark.

He could at least still sense their bodies with his mind. They began to make a circle around him. Jordan lifted his first victim off the ground and began spinning him around the room. He used the man's body to strike the others—the first, second, and third—until they were all down and out. Mary Ann Miller pushed more numbers, and he could sense Jillian falling to the floor.

"If you do not stop, Jordan, I will kill her. Do you have it within you to let her die?" Mary Ann asked.

"No, but you clearly have it in you, Aunt Clara." Jordan began to disassemble the device within her hand. She screamed as her hand expanded and contracted until it exploded from the internal pressure. Small fragments of her hand were left about the room in a bloody mess like a semi-exquisite Picasso painting. Jordan ran to where Jillian had collapsed and held her in his arms.

"Jillian . . . Jillian?" He kept repeating as he quietly wept, "Please don't leave me." He felt for a pulse. It was faint, but it was there. Mary Ann Miller writhed in pain on the floor. Jillian slowly regained consciousness.

"Jordan . . . what happened?"

"Freedom, Jillian, we gained our freedom. Now lie still." Jordan set Jillian gingerly back on the ground and went to Mary Ann. As he walked over to Mary Ann, he began to take off his shirt, and he wrapped it around the place where her hand once was. "We have to get you to a hospital."

Mary Ann scoffed and asked, "Why would you help me?" She still had a hint of insanity in her eyes.

"Because you are my aunt Clara."

CHAPTER 5

AT BETHESDA HOSPITAL, Jordan's temperature continued to rise. At the emergency entrance, Jordan dropped off Jillian and Clara to be attended to. "How will I reach you?" Jillian asked with deep concern for his well-being.

"The Internet, I will contact you through the Internet."

Jillian thought that was a strange answer, but he pulled her in close to kiss her deep. "I love you, Jordan. I always have," she said.

"I love you too, Jillian." He stroked her gold-spun velvet hair one last time, careful not to burn her skin with his own. His body was reaching a critical temperature, and as he walked away from Jillian and the hospital, his skin began to smoke and char like red embers. His skin began to burn off his own body. There was no sound as flesh fell from his body or screams of agony as the inferno that was his body burned him alive. A silver glow began to appear under the flames that were now barely recognizable as Jordan. He quickly began to melt into a puddle of bio-nanobytes that were still alive, but they lay there motionless.

Jillian couldn't take her eyes away from the carnage that was the love of her life. She simply sat there outside the hospital in utter shock and disbelief. She could do nothing but cry as an orderly emerged from the hospital to help with Mary Ann.

"Mama! Are you okay!" The frantic woman was clearly Mary Ann's daughter. She looked at Jillian and asked, "What happened to her hand!" Jillian could barely tell her that it blew up, but the woman must not have believed her because she asked again, "What happened to her hand!"

"It blew up!" Jillian said again, this time as a matter-of-fact. Mary Ann, who was in and out of consciousness, asked where Jordan was. Jillian responded while still weeping, "He melted, Mary Ann. You caused him to burn and melt!" Jillian could feel the rage building in her as she was beginning to accept that what had happened was even real.

"Oh good," Mary Ann began to say. "I thought he may have died." "I just told you he burned and melted to the ground! Of course, he died!"

"I know, dear. I heard you. He isn't dead. He's evolving. I wonder to what this time. You can bet that whatever he is next, he will still protect you, Jillian. He loved you, you know. We made him that way," she said as she let out a small yelp from the pain.

Jillian raced to where the puddle had been, expecting to see something, anything. Yet there was no puddle and no Jordan. As she collapsed on the ground from exhaustion and grief, she couldn't help but remember his last words to her. He promised to reach her on the Internet. All she could do was smile as she thought, *I really must check my e-mail.*

The End

*Honor, friendship, honesty, and bravery and with a quest in
life to be someone or a part of something greater than ourselves.
In our imagination are the beginnings of lives true future.*

—Arthur C. Jett
September 18, 2014

STERLING GRAY PARANORMAL INVESTIGATOR

ARTHUR C JETT

TABLE OF CONTENTS

THE BOOK

SURE, IT'S ALL sunny and bright in California. There are smiles for miles, that is, until someone puts a knife in your back. The beautiful coast, it's something to see from the beach to the redwoods, or at least what's left of them. Maybe go to LA to see the smog, fun times. Good old home sweet home. Oh, how I miss her. Just reminiscing, just a short break from—you got it—the book. No ordinary book, of substantial substance, to the right people. Both the good and bad want it. Fantastic and unimaginable are the treasures that lie within and doom and upheaval, disorder and pandemonium, if the context is even slightly misconstrued. Incantations or its enchantments will bring not only folly but also death to its unsuspecting reader.

The book had been locked away for the last five hundred years, and now someone had stolen it, stolen it from a priest at the all-suffering monastery just outside St. Rayes, California, far inland on the coast south of San Diego. The priest of the Suffering Order had been its caretaker for the last two centuries. Now somebody smart had found the book, somebody really smart, and now the earth was in trouble. From fires to flooding to entering subterranean and heaven, it was all there, as well as the passing of time and space. Creatures of all shapes and forms lay prey in its lines. The book was written by a collaboration of scholars of the light and darkness seeking the future and past witches and warlocks, those who sang incantations out loud. The title *Some Pictures* was penned by Wilford Giloc, who had put an inked quill to paper. He was a scholar and scientist who roamed the halls of Oxford in the mid- to late 1500s. His studies included the occult and the black arts as well as the strange and paranormal. He even studied potions and herbs from around the world. *Some Pictures* was a handbook, if you will, for the misunderstood. The power this book contained was vast and would be released upon the earth unless found and re-entombed, which is where I come in.

My name is Sterling Gray, and I am a paranormal detective. I specialize in the abnormal, spells, ghosts, and voodoos. Yep, that would be me. I was born in Bakersfield, California, to parents who were—for lack of a better word—gypsies from the Old Country. All those from the Old Country grew up traveling the country in old cars and travel trailers. Today the kids would be in what is referred to as homeschooling. County fairs, carnivals, and festivals—it's what gypsies do, or at least it's what my gypsy family did. Tonics and palm readings are what my family was known for. My dad was good at sleight of hand, and my mom, in her younger days, performed a hypnotic gypsy dance that seduced men and held them in a somewhat lewd trance. As my mother got older, she specialized in palm reading and danced less as time passed. The palm reading was a very lucrative business. Pop still did some slight-of-hand stuff and made some tonic sales until I was about fifteen. We finally settled in a small town outside San Francisco, where I attended San Bruno High School. Mom and Pop set up a palm reading office in town. This was where my mother flourished with her palmistry, or chiromancy, skills. Clients came from all over the world for her predictions to know their future. Her clients ranged from the common man or woman to politicians and celebrities alike. All were seeking her readings. She had some loyal customers who came two or three times a week for years. To me, it really seemed that she had mystical powers. You know, like a witch. Just by practicing palm reading and tarot cards, she had collected quite a few books on mysticism, spells, and herb uses of all kinds.

My pop was a jovial, happy-go-lucky guy. He loved to have fun, but my mother (more than once) would have to tell him to not play with something or to stop trying to have fun with something that I considered to be mystical. She took her work very seriously and was told that this magic was very dangerous. As I was growing up, I took her work and magic very seriously as well. I would spend countless hours reading books on black magic, spell books, and potion recipes.

Listing incantations was like a spelling bee for me. So that is how I grew up. After high school, I spent two years at Berkeley to study for a paranormal science degree and refine my skills, which was short-lived because of a four-year stint in the Marine Corps.

When my parents were killed in a car accident, I inherited the house and palm reading business. To this day, I still have many customers like my mother did before me. As you can guess, I also investigate paranormal activities, for a commanding price. Investigating is not cheap. When the Brothers of the Suffering Order called, all I needed to know was how much to expect for the job, where to start, which was the monastery, and who knew of the book and its powers. While loading up the 1969 Mercedes that was left to me by my mother, I made sure to pack all the tools of the trade. This included holy water, crosses, and several assortments of bullets for my 1911 Colt .45. I also made sure to pack some garlic, among other herbs, and some colorful crystals for decoration and professionalism. They looked good when laying everything out on the table.

The eight-and-a-half-hour drive was long and tiring. The drive from San Bruno to St. Rayes was almost six hundred miles. When I arrived, I met the head abbot and exchanged pleasantries. The monastery was a three-story building made of brick and cobblestone as were many of the churches in California. There were only fourteen Brothers of the Suffering Order left who lived at and maintained the monastery. Out of those fourteen, only two knew of the book's existence, the abbot and the keeper. The keeper cared for several pieces of artifacts. Abbot Noland, the keeper, was a short, round, and bald man who seemed to be distinguished and a little angry.

The book had been gone for twenty-four hours. Time was critical. The book was leaking spells and time warps as was evident by a large hole in the basement wall. The hole was a portal, a portal to hell. They were lucky that most demonic entities were just too stupid to find their way out. It was part of their hell, I suppose. No traces of ectoplasm or unearthly activities surrounded the portal either. The abbot and I would have to work fast to seal the portal with my trusted book of spells and incantations. I had written this book over my lifetime of studies and, in all honesty, what worked and didn't, along with some untested theories. So with the abbot performing his prayers, I recited a spell to turn the portal back onto itself. The goal was to turn it into a sort of U-turn, and once a demonic spirit found the portal and used it. They would simply step through it straight back into hell. I think it goes without saying, but those tortured souls are in hell for a reason, and most have come to expect conundrums such as this spell.

After further assessing the area around the portal, I could tell that not much other magic had spilled out of the book except for some beautiful flowers that were growing along the wall in the basement. The flowers were lush and appeared to be from a rainforest. This was occurring because both good and evil magic was leaking out of the ancient parchment. Beauty could spring from its pages just as fast as the portal had.

All the abbots were accounted for, but the book was gone. There was no strange behavior to suggest any of them had anything to do with the missing book. The book had been kept in a large cottonwood tree that had been grown specifically to house the book. When the tree was between fifteen and twenty years old, a slot was cut into the tree to house a box made of iron. Over the years, the tree grew around the box, encasing it in the trunk. The tree provided shade for the courtyard of the monastery. Whoever had taken the book cut into the tree to remove the box and opened the portal in the basement to either make their escape or use it as a diversion. The more I thought about it, the more I thought it was the latter of the two. The person who took the book was not aware of its full potential power or the danger it would bring.

I had done all I could at the monastery to fix things, so I began to roll a chained crystal over where the book was housed to gather a sense of what direction it was headed in, which worked great. The crystal pulled due north, which meant it did not enter the portal and reconfirmed my leakage theory. Abbot Noland insisted on going with me to find the book, but I insisted that he remain at the monastery in case there were more abnormal activities that occurred. He agreed.

The chained crystal hung on the rearview mirror of my Mercedes as I pulled away from the monastery. As I drove, the crystal began to rock north to south, with the heavier pull being due north still. By now, it was getting late as I pulled back onto I-5 North St. Rayes in the Tiguan River Valley. I stopped at the first exit I could find to refuel the car and myself. I spent $33 on the fuel and another $20 on beef jerky, Cheetos, and a large Red Bull. These were a mainstay of my deductive powers. I needed to stay awake as long as I could. The thief already had a twenty-four-hour head start.

Once I was back on the road, the crystal kept pulling north past San Diego. I continued my drive up along the coast of California, and by daybreak, I was in Santa Clarita, California, just north of LA. The Red Bull had worn off, and I was running on no sleep, so I decided to pull off the road into a rest area, roll the windows down, and shut the car off. I then crawled into my back seat to lie down at around five fifty in the morning and slept until almost noon. I awoke to the thumping noise of the crystal bouncing off the windshield of my Mercedes. The power of the book was strong. I climbed out of the back of my car, half dehydrated from the sun baking my car. I covered my eyes to shield them from the late morning sun and made my way to the head, did my business, washed my hands and face, and gargled with the Listerine I kept in my glove box. I then bought a cup of coffee from a vending machine for $1.25, which, even for such a small cup, I thought was a good deal.

As I drove north on the freeway, I noticed the traffic was quite heavy, but as I rolled through the ocean of cars and the noon sun began to fade overhead, I began to make good time. The air became much clearer as I drove north in beautiful California. Even with all the rat racing of life here, there is still nowhere I would rather live, but something felt not quite right here, and I meant something physical wasn't right. As only my trained eye could see, there was a wobble in time and space. It started as a little glitch, the clock in the car would jump back and forth, and there would be just split-second movements in the sky, kind of like you were looking in a carnival mirror. It was a sickening look between time. The rolling ocean waves and the horizon would feel ever so slightly different to a large ship crew. Yes, there it was, a slight ping in time. The book was right here not too long ago, maybe just an hour or two ago. The crystal still beat in a steady rhythm due north, so on I drove, the mile markers passing me by one by one. It was important to try and keep track of them. I didn't want to get caught in a time loop and continuously pass by mile marker 120 and over again.

If the book had been opened, it could spell disaster for a lot of people. Up until now, it had remained closed, and with some luck, it would hopefully stay that way. As I drove farther north, I began studying my surroundings—the land, air, and people I would pass by. The people were so oblivious to their space, some were talking to themselves, some were singing old favorites that were playing on the radio while tapping a beat and bobbing their head up and down. They seemed like hallucinogenic chickens forever locked in their rolling cages. There were families completely unaware of what was going on in their own backyards. There were children making faces and often gestures from their windows of life. Rich and poor, new and old vehicles whooshing through the intervals of reality and their advancing progress in space—even if you just slightly observe life in motion, you could pick up on the nuances and patterns. Its colors, the rough and smooth ebbs and flows of inanimate objects such as hats, air freshener, the rubber of the tires on the road almost always blending together to create seamless fortune that is our lives.

MORTROK

THE DRIVE NORTH was long and hot. The morning faded from cool mountain running to hot valley floor. The crystal kept true north. Somewhere around Los Banos, California, I pulled into an old mom-and-pop gas station. The car needed fuel, and so did I. There were no notable occurrences after filling the Mercedes with premium fuel because that was what my mom always used. It was a little family tradition I keep alive for her. "Premium fuel for a premium car" was what she would say when we put fuel in the car together. I sat in the car for a few moments, thinking of her and my father, my strange and weird parents, and how much I missed them and still was amazed at how much I still loved them. The crystal continued to pull north, and now so did the Mercedes. I hadn't driven very far when I noticed a dark cloud along the roadside. It looked like exhaust fumes from a diesel truck but different. It was maybe two hundred yards ahead, and it was swirling like a sideways tornado. I pulled just past it and stopped. As I looked back in the rearview mirror, there was a dark figure walking out of the smoke. It was a man of medium build. He approached the car, and as he did, I rolled the passenger window down.

"Are you all right, friend?" I asked as he started to pass by the car. He stopped and first stood there. Upon looking at him in more detail, I noticed that his clothes were layering in a fabric I did not recognize. He wore a big floppy hat. As a matter of fact, he looked like Galileo or someone straight from the thirteenth or fourteenth century. Maybe a professor or scholar of the time.

I reached and opened my door and motioned for him to come in. As he entered the passenger side of the car, I could smell the smoke. His body and clothes reeked of it. He simply sat in the seat and did not move, so I motioned to him to close the door. I powered the old car back onto the freeway. As I did, the smoke began to pour out of the car for a short way, and then it eventually faded away. The passenger's eyes were wide with amazement, or maybe it was fear. I wasn't quite sure.

Then out of nowhere, he said, "Nice car, man." My jaw unhinged. You see, I knew he was from the past, that somehow he was from the book. He looked at me and said, "Don't trip, man. I've been here before. Yep, this isn't my first rodeo. Cowboy '69, right?" He was referring to the '69 SL Mercedes.

"Yeah," I said in almost shock. "It's a '69 SL Mercedes."

"Yeah, I know. It's a very fine machine."

"My name is Sterling, but most people call me Stew. What's your name?

"My name is Mortrok, and most people call me Mortrok, but you can call me Maury. It goes better with the times."

"Okay, where are you headed, Maury?"

"Same place you are, Stew. I'm going after the book."

"So you are from the past?"

"Yes, I was born in 1435, but I am not coming from the past. I am coming from the future."

"You can time travel?"

"Yes, and it is a good thing too because it was really hot where I came from. House fire. I almost had the book, but then I had to bail. The house fire was too hot. Your 'time travel,' as you call it, is not an exact art, but over the years, I have gotten better at knowing where to go and when."

"So you were looking for me?"

"Yep, tried for the car twice, but I kept missing, which meant I had to keep going back into the fire. So I shot for the side of the road in hopes you would see me, you being seen ahead and all. I took a chance you would stop for me."

"So on with our adventure to save the good world as opposed to the bad world?"

"You are absolutely correct in your assumption, Mr. Gray, or can I call you Stew?"

"Stew is fine. Well, Maury, I am in search of the book. Do you know of the book?"

"Yes, of course. It is my home. Pages 412 through 415 are mine. It is where my magic and myself reside, but something happened, and I fell from the book, so I must retrieve it to go home. My magic is very limited outside of the book, but I do have some spells for time shifting and a few other things up my sleeves. I can only return home if I am touching the book. And you, Stew, what is your purpose for the book?"

"Only to return it to the Brothers of the Suffering Order for safekeeping."

"So you are a seer with mystical connections, Stew?"

"Yes, I am a paranormal detective."

"And your parents were channelers of the mystic world?"

"They were gypsies from the Old World."

"Of course, they were," said Maury.

"Do you often time travel?" asked Stew.

"Very rarely," answered Maury. "I love living in the book, as do the others."

"Others?" asked Stew.

"Oh yes, there are many others who live in the book. Some are good and some bad. The good ones choose to live there. The bad ones . . . well, let's just say that most of them that are in the book are trapped there, and it's for the best."

"How is it that you are out of the book, Maury?"

"Some odd chance of fate, I suppose. Maybe the book was dropped and opened to my pages accidentally, but I think it just may have leaked me out along the way. As I am sure you have seen the disturbances in the atmosphere, one thing is for sure, Stew, we have to retrieve that book soon, or there will be hell to pay on Earth and beyond."

"Are you saying there could be universal consequences?"

"Well, yes, that would be what I was saying." The crystal kept a steady beat in a northbound direction.

"So, Maury, tell me about the house fire you escaped from twice."

"Yes, the fellow who has the book set the fire. Quite by accident, I am sure. I shifted into the house both times, just a little too late to stop him."

"Where was this house, Maury?"

"Just north of Bakersfield, a little town called Oildale. I think we are an hour or two away from there."

"Tell me about the man that has the book."

Maury began to tell of a younger man in his mid- to late twenties, about six feet tall with dark hair and light green eyes. He looked like he could be about 160 pounds. He was wearing a white shirt, a blue jacket, and blue jeans with dirty white tennis shoes. The way he moved and sounded was very erratic, but Maury was sure it was from the effects of the book. I was interested in all Maury had to tell. Attention to detail was very important.

The midafternoon heat was extreme. As we followed the crystal up I-5 and down the long grapevine mountain to the valley floor below, we crept closer and closer to Oildale. Only thirty miles left. We talked of odd and strange occurrences that lamented with the past and the present as if we were old friends. He told me how he could only leave the book for a short period, one or two days at most, usually about every ten years if he desired. He had said in the beginning how much he would look forward to his pilgrimage into the real world, but over time, he preferred the many magical realms of the book for journeying deep within the dark magic, with its mythical creatures and bright array of colors to stimulate one's mind and sense, to sail with swashbuckling pirates on stormy seas in the search of endless treasures, to soar above giant and majestic mountains of distant planets in far-off universes that shone of green and gold, the warm winds that blew through your soul to rejuvenate your spirit from an orange desert that was as intoxicating as a bottle of fine wine. These were just a few places you could travel in the book.

Maury continued on to say "I am not the only living being in the pages. Esmeralda, the queen of the purple magic, can also be found throughout the book. Purple is almost always used for good . . . almost. She is so beautiful that my heart aches for her still today. Her beauty makes all the other colors of the rainbow shy away except for purple, which all her powers come from. Her magic can be found throughout the book. Her magic reaches far beyond the pages into this world. I would daresay she is watching us as we speak."

Maury and I finally reached Oildale, California, and pulled up to the aforementioned house or what was left of it. It was burned to the ground. The crystal was still pulling north, which meant the book was no longer here. We got out of the car and walked past the yellow tape that surrounded the property that was placed there by the fire department. I looked at Maury and noticed that he was still wearing the same smoke-choked clothes as before.

"Maury, remind me to get you some clean clothes. I have extra in the back of the car."

Maury started to fuss for a moment, but he then caved and accepted. We pushed our way through the burned rubble from the destruction of the fire. There was nothing left to indicate the book had ever been there except for some vines that had blossomed in what was left of the center of the house.

Oildale seemed quaint and rustic, but looks can be deceiving, and something was telling me that we should be on our way. I retrieved some clothes for Maury—a pair of shorts, a T-shirt, and an old but clean pair of tennis shoes. Everything I gave him was roughly one to two sizes too big, but I was pretty sure Maury wouldn't know the difference. In fact, he said, "I have worn many hats throughout my life—physician's skullcap worn by the clans, bicorn from the French army and one of my favorites, as well as britches, trousers, and overalls from around the world—but never a Bart Simpson T-shirt and an Oakland A cap." And here I was sitting next to a four-hundred-year-old, black-magic-practicing wizard who also traveled through time. He also had a girlfriend named Esmerelda, who was a purple magic queen in search of a book in which they, and others, lived. It was turning out to be a pretty good day, or at least that was what I thought.

DARK BLUE FIRE

THE FIRE HAD burned hot, something I had missed. I couldn't put my finger on it. The coals had been dark blue in color. "Maury, what started this house fire?"

"I don't know. It was burning when I shifted closer to the book the first time. The second time, the house was just smoldering, and I remember a lot of them had a red light. That's why I shifted to the roadside, where you found me and picked me up. There is something else. In the book, there are beasts, much like dragons, who spew dark blue fire. They are very dangerous."

"Could one of the beasts have gotten out?"

"Maybe. Those of us who live in the book call them drogs! They are usually shy, but when provoked, they can become very unpleasant. As a matter of fact, their blue flame burns incredibly hot. The only ones I am aware of these days are owned by Perkio, an ancient warrior wizard. He is a truly bad man. He was imprisoned by his king many years ago. As long as he remains in the book, the world will remain safe."

As we drove north toward Westerville, I couldn't help but feel there was plenty Maury wasn't telling me. We continued to find more fires along the roadside as we traveled along I-5. Orange gate, orange stand, the old Zion zoo until there was a large black dog dragon with wings, and it was spitting fire like it was chewing tobacco. We rolled into the parking lot just to the side of the juice stand, and the drog looked at us right away. As he did, a light blue fire spittle dripped from his mouth, and his eyes were a darker blue. The ears of the creature were at least ten inches long. His features reminded me of those of a werewolf, with wings about eight feet long, a spiked ridge along its back, and large claws like a lion. It just stood there at first as we looked into one another's eyes like some kind of children's games to see who would blink first, and it must have been me. The drog leaped for the car, and I threw it in reverse, but I was not fast enough. The drog's front claws landed on the front bumper as he let out a burst of blue flame. It seemed like it lasted ten seconds or more. The flame singed the top of the car. Maury began yelling out an incantation. The drog jumped straight into the air. This time I knew it was going to come in through the windshield, but miraculously, just before it landed, it turned into a butterfly and fluttered off.

I looked at Maury and said, "Good job, man."

"Don't get too happy. It only lasts a few minutes. Then it will turn back into a really mad drog. I am not sure how long it will last out of the book after it turns back into a drog. One good thing is that there was no Perkio!" Just then, something flashed in the distance. "Look! More blue flames! We need to head in that direction," Maury said with authority.

I did not argue the point. The flames were on a small hill just off to our right. The old Mercedes crackled as it rolled slowly up the road. As we approached, we could see another drog, but this one was moving slowly, leaning back and forth until finally, it stopped and fell over sideways. It lay there for a moment, and then it disintegrated into a bright blue light, and then there was nothing left.

"That's what happens when they are out of the book too long." "What about you?" I asked.

"The same thing," he solemnly replied, "except I have magic . . . It helps me stay here longer. Mind you, it's not much longer, only two or three days if I am lucky, yes, if I am *very* lucky. You see, I need to get back into the book soon, or well, you have seen my indubitable fate."

"Then we should get moving!" I said.

The crystal tapped on the windshield, still in a northern pull. The top of the Mercedes had a pretty good scorch mark on it, but it did not affect its performance. There it was again, that feeling that Maury wasn't telling me the whole truth. We rode in silence. We made our way over to I-5 from Oildale. The heat of the day was getting extreme, well over one hundred degrees. The air conditioner worked well even when the temperatures would reach these extremes. The old Mercedes would get hot, but I prided myself on maintaining the family heirloom. The heat felt like a furnace blasting away next to us. The horizon often looked as if it were melting. A watery mirage in a not-so-far-away future.

"It's cooler in the book," Maury said with a tone of sadness in his voice, much like a homesick child who was off to a summer camp for the first time. The reality of potentially not returning to the book was beginning to set in, and he seemed as if he was pondering his own mortality. Maybe it was the perishability, Esmerelda, or the loss of his home in the book.

The crystal moved again, still ticking toward the north. The radio was a welcome relief from this stress or at least a reassurance of my reality. My whole life had been steeped in many different realms of magic, which included mind reading and things as far out as you are able to believe. So rock on, Creedence Clearwater Revival. As the miles melted off the road, Maury and I rocked on.

"Maury," I asked, "are you hip to rock and roll?"

He answered, "Of course! I have loved rock since the '50s. In the 1800s, I rocked out to Ludwig van Beethoven and Wolfgang Amadeus in the 1700s. I was there when this car first came on the scene in 1969 and even before that when Harley and Davidson came out with motorbikes. I was there in Kitty Hawk, North Carolina, when the Wright Brothers flew their first plane. Yes, I have been to a lot of firsts."

We drove on through the day. The sun finally made its way below the amber horizon, and as it did, the air around us cooled to a bearable temperature, somewhere in the eighties. Tired didn't truly describe the way I felt after ten hours of driving, even in a Mercedes-Benz. We pulled off to a little roadside motel.

Maury asked, "What are you doing, Stewy?"

"I need some rest, Maury. I can't keep going like this. I will end up killing us. How about you, Maury? Do you sleep at all in the book?"

"No, not really. It's more like dreaming while awake."

"Okay, well, I just need a few hours to sleep."

"That might be too long though. If I don't get back to the book, I will die. I will drive, Stewy. You can sleep in the passenger seat."

"You know how to drive?"

"Of course. Now come on, let's get going."

As we changed places, a large blue fireball shot across the sky over our heads, and then another lit up the sky after that. I yelled, and as I did, Mortrok spoke an incantation, and a force field rose around us. Mortrok then fired a red ball of energy back at the attackers and took one drog down. Two to go. The brilliant light with exploding the drog still illuminated. A second drog jumped from behind a car in front of the hotel office, smashing into the force field. Maury fired off another red fireball, catching the menacing drog in the face, and the third moved to our right. Snarling, its fiery blue eyes were trained on us. The blue spittle dripped from his fangs.

"My forcefield won't last much longer!" Maury said as he fired another red ball of energy that cleanly missed its target. "That's it, Stewy! Plain out!" The drog seemed to know it as he let out a growl in our direction.

"Can't you turn them into a butterfly or something? Or how about a frog? That's pretty close to a drog, right?"

"I can try! Act for me, drog. Go turn into a frog." The incantation seemed to have little to no effect.

"Is that it, Maury? Is that all you got?"

"Well, yeah. Do you have anything, Stewy?"

"None of that killer shit that you have."

"Nothing even with all of that training you have? Come on, Stewy, we need something now!"

"I call on freon a chilla, freon the beast, freon a chilla!" As the drog hit the forcefield, it began its circling again.

"Come on, Stewy, try again! He is still warm-blooded!"

"OK! Freon a chilla, with his concentration freon chilla!"

The drog stopped in his tracks, frozen. Then as if someone hit him with a sledgehammer, the drog shattered into a million tiny shards of crystal.

"Well, Stewy, how's it feel to know that your magic works?"

"It was the wrong incantation, and I didn't think it would really work."

"Stewy, you just lack confidence in yourself. The knowledge is there. You just have to believe in it. Embolden yourself. You are going to have to. The book is dangerous, so to return it, you must consider yourself a first-class wizard, a magician extraordinaire. It's going to take all your powers and strength. There's something there, all right?" Mortrok said as he glanced at the drogs. "There are so many drogs lost. I fear their master has something to do with this."

Back on the road, we stopped for gas and decided to check the oil and wash the windows of the Mercedes as well. I had my confidence, shaken for the first time in all my years I had faced a demon and won. I didn't feel very strong, though, and wondered what would happen when I came face-to-face with a witch or another danger of a higher level, a talisman that could affect the elements and the very soul of the earth. I shook it off, went to go use the restroom, and purchased some essentials for the road—two Red Bulls and a bag of some crunchy Cheetos. At this point, I felt like I lived on them.

"Maury, do you want something to eat or drink for the road?"

"Some wine and cheese would be fine."

I went back in and purchased more Red Bull and Cheetos and a big bag of beef jerky just to round out the meal. As we drove north to the tap of the crystal and the Red Bull kicked in, Maury began to tell me more about his life in the book as life ever after in the books. He talked about moving through the pages and meeting and enjoying his many friends, especially Queen Esmeralda, as she seemed to capture most of his attention. But there were many more, such as Gen. Li Chen, who had, as a much younger man, traveled the world, including the Caribbean, where he led his men to war against the island people. But these islanders were no ordinary islanders. Mambo voodoo laid waste to his army and captured the general. Li Chen was made a slave to the voodoo. He was entranced for a century before gaining access to the dark voodoo powers before he became the most powerful mambo chief of all time and ruled there for another century before being captured in the book by Wilford Giloc, the author of the book.

An accidental incantation was performed while Giloc was on holiday in the Caribbean. Giloc did not realize that his incantation was capturing the voodoo chief, and six months later, he discovered the chief, or Gen. Li Chen, was even living in the booklet alone, possessing magic in the book. Li Chen was free to be Li Chen, a five feet three inches man, not a six feet six inches voodoo chieftain raining havoc on local islanders. Li Chen wanted very much to just play chess and live out his days in the book. No conquering countries, no more death, and no destruction. He could be just a simple man in a quiet place.

"Li Chen has, over the years, become a close friend, if that is possible, in our world. Yes, I must return. I would miss my old friend in any case, so it is yet another reason to return to the book."

The car rumbled on, always north as if it were being drawn to the aurora borealis by its magnetic pull. Far into Northern California now, the Red Bull was again wearing off. The many hours of travel were taking a toll on me. I continued to watch for signs we were getting closer, but nothing yet. I wasn't seeing any signs of witchcraft or magic spells that might have leaked out of the book.

"We should get you some rest, Sterling, before you fall asleep and kill us both from behind the wheel."

"You are right, Maury."

The sign "Rest Area Two Miles" on the side of the roadside was where I would stop for some much-needed rest. It had been fourteen hours since I had left the Brothers of Sorrow Monastery. The battle with the drogs had also taken its toll. Maury AKA Mortrok looked no worse for wear. We pulled into the rest stop. I climbed into the back seat and passed out. I was not sure for how long I was asleep, but it felt like a vast dreamscape. It was the book of which I dreamed, the exotic places of the earth and space—Petra in Jordan, Malta with its bridges of grand vein of its cliff cities, and the red rock canyon of Utah, deep in the rainforest to see the commanding canopies—as far as the constellations of space and the planets of Mars, Mercury, Neptune, and the serpent's head and tail of the Serpents Capoda Aquila, Orion Aries. My imagination shuttered by its overwhelming inexplicable and inconceivable grandiose grandeur. The ice rivaled Neptune to melting sand of Mercury. My dreams were real or perhaps a spell from the book or hypnosis brought on by a clever magician. Dangling through time and space, trying to retire his life in a book, this book was becoming all-consuming. Suddenly, I was awoken by the gait of Mercedes rolling slowly up the dirt road. According to the placement of the sun, it must have been noon. Sleep had held me at bay for at least ten hours. To my surprise, Maury was driving, although I should not have been with his knowledge of modern-day technologies.

"Where are we?" I asked, downplaying reestablishing consciousness.

He replied, "Oregon, just north of Gramis pass. The crystal has shifted west."

"How long was I out?" I asked.

"Ten to twelve hours. Do you need to stop?"

"Yes, nature is calling me."

"Yes, Stewy, nature is truly calling all of us."

The Mercedes stopped on the side of the road like a trusted old milk horse at its next delivery point. A clay road lay like a Band-Aid in what looked to be a thick pine forest, which was reluctant to let the light of the sun dance through its wavering foliage. As I returned to the car, Maury said, "I believe the book to be close, up the road to the best of my recollection." A loud explosion shook the earth. A large shock wave ensued. The fabric of time and space hobbled past us. Again, another explosion and more bending of space before our eyes. Maury spoke in a quiet voice, "Time bombing, I've seen and heard it before. Perkio, he must be out of the book. It would explain the drogs along our path. The time bombs are from when he was going in and out of different periods such as the Iron Age, Early Modern Age, and the Cold War, just to give you an idea of where he is going and coming from. Now the explosions you hear are of when he tore the time continuum of the fabric of space, which then causes the wobble or bending in space. Why Perkio is bombing, I do not know, but isn't going to be good."

We traveled a little bit further in the Mercedes-Benz up the dirt road. We came to a small clearing. In the clearing, there in the Keystone Canyon were tanks along with two drogs, which appeared to be guarding the old war antiques. We stopped the Mercedes about two hundred yards from the clearing off the road in the woods.

PERKIO DESIGN

MAURY AND I made our way to just outside of the clearing. There were small blue flames all around the clearing. Then another loud explosion roared, and it was accompanied by a bright light. Once the light dimmed, I could see that Perkio was truly there, standing inside a large bubble three feet off the ground with his back to us. Two drogs, with blue flames leaking from their mouths and nostrils, ran to either side of the bubble. The drogs leaped with joy as their master spoke something to them softly like some beloved family house pet. The drogs looked more like puppies now rather than monsters of doom. We kept a concerned and watchful eye on them as we crept closer until one of the drogs stopped and looked straight at us. Perkio raised his head slightly, and then he said without missing a beat, "Mortrok, I see you have also escaped the book."

Mortrok stood quietly while considering his next words. "No, I have not escaped the book. I was dislodged maybe but not escaped. What are you doing, Perkio?"

"What does it look like I am doing? I am preparing for war against this world!"

Mortrok laughed and said, "With some swords, old tanks, and a few drogs?"

"It is a start, Mortrok."

With that, he whirled in a half circle and released the drogs. They came at us like insane greyhounds chasing down half-eaten mechanical rabbits that were tearing down the track at San Clarita. They were fast, all right. They crossed the clearing in a matter of seconds. Maury reached into his coat pocket and produced a silvery powder, which he then just blew into the air in front of us. The drogs froze in their tracks, blue flames dripping from their skulls. Perkio calmly jumped from the bubble and slowly walked to a pile of swords. He held out his hands over the pile, and suddenly, two swords flew into his hands as if they were possessed. He then began to spin around in circles.

"Who is this that you have with you, Mortrok?"

"His name is Sterling Gray, and he is a very powerful sorcerer from this time that may provide us access back into the book."

"For us, Mortrok? No, for yourself maybe. I am here to defeat this world and rule it for myself. Besides, not everyone wants to live in that dusty old book like you, Esmeralda, Li, and the others. Here is where we belong and where we should rule."

"You've been spending too much time with the drogs, Perkio. You, just like the rest of us, can only exist in the book. Being here, this can only be temporary, as you should well know."

"Is that so, Mortrok? Or is there something different this time?"

"What are you talking about, Perkio? What is it that has your mind reeling with madness this time? Is it the thought of power over the rest of the worlds, or is it just a short-man complex?" Perkio's eyes were the size of silver dollars, and he released the swords while he was still spinning. They flew toward us at a furious pace. Maury yelled, "Alcantore!" and lifted the drogs into the spinning swords' paths. One sword ricocheted into the ground and the other into the air away from us. Perkio kept advancing toward us. "Stop, Perkio! I do not want to kill you! I just want to return you to the book!"

"Then I should rather die if your magic can kill me!"

Perkio waved his hands, and two more swords flew at us, and with another wave of his hand, the tanks began to turn slowly in our direction. Again, Maury lifted the frozen drogs as a defense to help deflect the swords. The tanks stopped moving, and there was a moment of silence before a booming blast erupted from the tank's cannon. The 105 howitzer shell flew between Maury and me, landing some hundred yards past us. Still, we were thrown from our feet because of the explosion. The world went quiet and slowed to a snail's pace after we were knocked down. Even though I could not hear his words, I saw white lightning flying from Maury's hands that seemed as powerful as a winter storm. Still feeling like time was slowed down, I watched the attack as it traveled across the clearing and struck Perkio. To my amazement, Perkio seemed to take in the unbound energy. As Maury released Perkio, he fell to the ground. Perkio again waved his hands, but this time toward the ground. A blue energy shield shot across the clearing, striking the drogs down from the sky and out of the catatonic state. To my surprise, the two devil dragons retreated to and entered the bubble. Perkio began to levitate, and he too entered the bubble.

"This isn't over, Mortrok. Soon, the earth and the book shall be mine!" With that unceremonious departure, Perkio was gone.

"That was closer than I would have liked," said Mortrok. "His powers are growing, but what I would like to know is how he was released from the book. Someone, or something, is releasing the book's captives."

"When you say captives, are they being held there against their will?"

"Yes, most were imprisoned there for their wrongdoings, but for most, it was their salvation."

"Was it your salvation, Maury?"

"Yes, indeed it was. Until the book, there was only the dark side of my despair and the treachery and the promise of pain. That such as Perkio is filled with, a misguided soul ruled by a darker force which has turned his heart to stone. This plan to take over the earth is also the aspiration of others that are in the book. Wilford Giloc looked to remove these people and their evils from this earth by capturing them in the book. Think of it like rehab for bad spirits. Some chose death, and I chose the book after a while. I considered it a second chance at life. I wanted to feel like I could do something good."

Another boom rang out. It sounded like it was coming from two or three miles away. It had to be Perkio. He was moving toward the book by time bombing. If he doesn't find it soon, he will die, which means the book will die, or at least the part with Perkio shall die.

"Is that such a bad thing?" I admonished. "That character did not seem like part of the book that I wanted to read."

"You are wrong, Sterling! Because without people like Perkio, we would not know the evils of the world and we wouldn't understand the meaning of redemption. In other words, we would not get the full story that the book has to offer, and as am I, so is Perkio. He is already within the book for all to read." We walked back to the Mercedes.

"Maury, where exactly in the book do you think Perkio was released from?"

"I'm not entirely sure. My best guess would be where we first saw the drogs."

Tick tick tick. The crystal continued tapping the windshield, showing us the way down the road and then up along a smaller dirt road. We followed the directions the crystal provided for several miles until we came to a larger crossroad on top of the mountain. We then took a hard left onto another dirt road, which we could tell was well used. Soon, we came to another highway. *Tick tick tick.* The crystal continued tapping its directions against the windshield. We took a right. The forest trees still rose into the sky like towering skyscrapers, uniformly positioned as if to portray a city planner's dream. Every once in a while, another sonic boom would sound in the distance. Perkio, no doubt, was continuing his chase for the book. Yes, his time bombing was starting to seem random at best.

We traveled until we came to Eugene, where we checked into a Motel 6. It had been an eight-hour drive out of the mountains, and I was exhausted. Between fighting Perkio and the drogs and the travel, we both needed rest. There was no time for a shower; there was only time for my head to hit the pillow. By 7:00 a.m., I was up and grabbing a shower and getting dressed. Maury and I grabbed something to eat at a local diner called Green Fried Tomatoes. The coffee was hot, and the biscuits and gravy weren't bad either. We heard small talk from the locals of strange lights in the sky followed by a particular cracking thunder in the air.

We stopped at the 7-Eleven on our way out of town for Red Bull and gas. It was going to be a long day. Maury and I talked about Perkio's plan to take over the earths. Wait, *earths?*

"Hold on, Maury. You just said *earths*, not *earth*. That's plural."

"That's right. I really do mean as in more than one." I stared at him in disbelief and then quickly realized that Mortrok wasn't looking all that fresh. His physical being seemed like it was deteriorating before his eyes. Motrok's skin seemed to be far paler than usual, and his mood and overall demeanor was lethargic at best. He needed to get to the book and return home soon.

The traffic was light on I-5, and the weather was partly cloudy with moments of sunshine. The road was dry, though, and for that, I was grateful. In the sky, we could see spots where Perkio had time-bombed. He had left small indentations in the sky. If we weren't looking for these spots, then we would never have seen them. Soon, we saw Perkio blast back into the sky, and just as quickly as he appeared, he vanished again and again.

Maury said, "We need to get ahead of him to stop him. He is tearing the fabric of time, and if it is too big of a tear, we won't be able to fix it." We pushed the Mercedes up to seventy-five miles per hour, and we began to pass him, but the problem was that he was zigzagging across the sky. We drove what we thought was about two miles ahead of Perkio, and Maury said, "Stop the car. This will have to work. Sterling, I will need your help for this spell. The plan is to throw a net across the sky to catch him if we are lucky. So just do what I do."

Mortrok began to chant and wave side to side. We chanted, "Our net to the sky so bird don't fly. Our net to the sky so bird don't fly." Over and over, we chanted this, and as we did, I could see a large blue energy net form about five hundred feet in the air, and it seemed to be about a quarter of a mile wide. We heard a loud blast a half mile out. It was Perkio. Then there was another blast just in front of the net as Perkio disappeared again. The net began to stretch as Maury yelled louder, "Our nets to the sky so bird don't fly." Then Maury yelled, "Throw your hand forward!" We did, and the net closed around Perkio's sphere. Perkio reappeared and this time threw something from the bubble toward us. It looked like a rock, but it was actually a grenade. As the grenade came closer and closer to us, it never exploded. Perkio hadn't pulled the detonation pin before throwing it. We could see that Perkio was figuring out why the grenade wasn't exploding as he used his powers to pull the pin on the grenade. I yelled to Maury and slammed him to the ground. We both knocked our heads against the ground as we fell. The bubble, still in the net, hit the ground as well at the same time that the grenade went off. The sphere filled with gray smoke with a light pink hue to it. The sphere soon fully collapsed, and as it did, the smoke dissipated. We could now see that all that was left of Perkio was a few large body parts drenched in the liquefied remnants of the rest of him. Perkio's design was over.

A LITTLE HELP FROM OUR FRIENDS

WE NEEDED TO find the book soon. Maury wouldn't last much longer. Maury also seemed quite upset that Perkio had died. After all, they had been neighbors for almost four hundred years, albeit Perkio was a crazy neighbor who wanted to rule the universe at all costs, even death and destruction. Nevertheless, Perkio had seemed like a permanent fixture in Maury's life, and he was feeling the loss. To try and cheer him up, I suggested that we try and contact some of the other characters in the book if that was even possible.

He said, "I will try transcendental meditation. Maybe that will work. I will try to contact Esmeralda. She and I are on a level to which we could possibly pick up on one another's thought patterns." So for the next fifteen minutes, Mortrok meditated. He tried to pick up something, anything, from the book, first with Esmeralda and then with Gen. Li Chen, to no avail. He finally stopped and said, "It's no use. The book is moving and moving quickly." We made our way back to the car and began as before to follow the crystal. Again, it tapped the windshield and led us north. "We must hurry, Sterling. There is not much time." We kept our eyes open for any sign of the book, for any wobbles, flashes, disruptions in the atmosphere, anything at all. There was nothing.

Back on I-5, the rain began to come down hard, so hard that the sky was so dark it looked like it was night already. The wind blew the car to the side, but I was able to control it. "We must push forward, Sterling. Every second counts." For what seemed like an eternity, the rain pounded the Mercedes as if someone stood on top of the car and poured buckets of water down on the windshield.

Forty-five minutes passed, and the wind and rain finally started to lighten just a bit. Maury seemed to come to life. "I feel the book. We are so close."

"How close is it?" I asked Maury.

"Close enough to try and time shift jump."

Before I could object, he was gone, vanished into thin air. No smoke or vapor, no wobble in time or space, just gone.

The rain had all but stopped as I pulled my car to the side of the road to try and gather myself. The crystal still tapped the windshield with a steady beat. I thought, *Okay, I must go on. The book is close, and after all, that is what I am after. It's my job.* But now there was this eerie feeling about my new friend Mortrok. Was he okay? Did he make it back to his home and friends he so loved? Those questions had to be answered and soon. The sun started to peek through the clouds a little. My journey must continue. The magic in me was growing stronger. I could feel myself absorbing it from the book and the air surrounding me. School had taught me plenty about the magic, and the sorcerers and magicians, and my family with all the Old World had taught them. They could not have prepared me for the overwhelming sensation of the magical power that was coming over me. This was different; this was supernatural. Had Maury left me something of a power lead, and had he transformed me somehow to channel the book's power or its inhabitants' magic? Whatever it was, Red Bull couldn't hold a match to it; the energy was exhilarating. Light began to emanate from my body; my eyes glowed turquoise. For what seemed like hours, the classic Mercedes glowed. Finally, it stopped. Now it was more important than ever to find the book.

As I thought this, a TV-sized screen appeared before my eyes. A vision perhaps? It showed me a small motorbike speeding down I-5. The rider had a knapsack on his back. The book was in the satchel. I could see it very clearly. Soon, I saw a mile marker in my vision, number 248, just outside Salem, Oregon, about one hundred miles ahead of me. So I pushed the old Mercedes just above the legal speed limit to try and make up some ground on the perpetrator of the crime that was so intertwined with my life now. Every fifteen or twenty minutes, I would check the vision to see how much time I was making up. The satchel was upon the back of the rider, which showed the book vividly but not the face of the thief. How I was able to have these visions and know the incantation to bring it forth was a little bit freaky but damn sure it has to do with the book and Maury.

As the Mercedes pushed north, the car began to fill with black smoke. A figure appeared next to me in the passenger seat. A very large black man with a deep bottom of the barrel baritone voice said, "I am Gen. Li Chen, master of voodoo! I am your sole master, if I do so wish it." I rolled down the windows to let the smoke escape, which was necessary as the smoke was filling the cabin. As the windows rolled down, Li Chen spoke and simply said, "You may." His head was up against the roof of the Mercedes, his knees pushing on the dash, and his hands looking like catcher's gloves with giant sausage fingers. A range of white dots ran the length of his huge head. It appeared to be some sort of tribal tattoo. A bald head and his clothes consisted of some type of vest that was too short, an armband with long feathers and glass beads, and red canvas jeans that were well worn and held up by a rope—hillbilly style. A ragged pair of sandals were worn on the biggest pair of feet I had ever seen.

"The book is where I come from, sent to help you retrieve it and bring it back to the Brothers of the Suffering Order."

"Okay, well, I'm Sterling, Sterling Gray. I go by Stewy."

"Yes, Mortrok sent me to help."

"Is Mortrok okay?"

"Yes, he is recovering in the book, but it is all for naught if we don't return the book."

"What do I call you? Li Chen?"

"Yes, Li Chen is fine. May I call you Stewy?"

"Yes, please do. We are not far from the book." I told Li Chen, voodoo chief. He was big and smelled like rum and chicken. His eyes were glazed over, white like milky-looking orbs.

Meanwhile, we continued on I-5 northbound going 70 mph in pursuit of the book and its captor. We hadn't driven very far when Li Chen asked, "Can I drive the car?"

"Do you even know how to drive a car?"

"No, but I would like to learn."

I thought it over and responded quietly so as not to rile him, "Then no, maybe later."

"Well, it is a very nice car."

"Thank you," I politely added. "It was my mother's." Suddenly, another vision happened, and I could see the rider of the motorcycle stopping on the side of the road. "There is only one guy, Li Chen. He still has the knapsack on with the book in it, but he's stopped riding, and he is taking the book out of the pack. Now he is opening the book. This must be how the contents are escaping." The vision then stopped, and I shook my head. "It will be another fifteen minutes before I can call on another vision. What could the rider have been looking for? Any ideas, Li Chen?"

"Well, what most seek is power from the book, but it can also provide wealth and, for some, much more life. Most choose power over the earths and beyond. There are also some spells that can conjure light or dark or even speed and strength. Immortality could be granted, but beasts of power also reside there. But for those who know not of these powers, it is dangerous for us all. There are built-in safeguards to protect the book and its inhabitants. Enchantments such as fire in the wrong hands could be let loose, and the reader may burst into flames themselves. We are clearly not dealing with someone who would trigger safeguards such as that. This person is able to handle it with care and release spells unto the world without harming themselves."

I sped the car up to 75 mph, which the street signs designated as the new speed limit. A few minutes later, I had another vision of the rider mounting his bike and working himself back onto I-5 North. We drove another hour, and there it was, a ten-foot-tall rock statue that was on the side of the road. People were trying to stop and take pictures with it. There were no police yet, but at least four cars had stopped. We pulled up to the side behind the other cars and walked to the base of the statue. Li Chen began to look very concerned the closer we came to the statue, and finally, he said, "It is a rolla!"

"What do you mean it is a rolla? What is that?"

"That is what this statue is called in the book, rolla. They are very dangerous. We should move the people back, *way* back."

"Why, what does he do—" Before I could finish my sentence, I got my answer. The statue began to move and quickly collapsed into the shape of a boulder, which then began to roll toward us. I began to yell at the crowd. "Get out of the way! It's coming straight for us. run!" The rolla was able to move much faster than I had expected. It started to move to the left and then to the right, and then it re-centered itself. Faster and faster, it came rolling over one car after another. People ran in every direction, including Li Chen and me.

"Up the hill!" I heard Li Chen yell. "They can't move uphill very well!" We started running toward the hill that Li Chen had pointed out, running on an uphill incline. The rolla struck another car, and then it hit a telephone pole. Li Chen turned as the rolla started up the hill. Li Chen halted, held his hands high in the air, and began to yell, "Oh, rolla, stand! Oh, rolla, stand! Oh, rolla, stand!" The boulder came to a stop just at the bottom of the incline and unfolded to become the statue again. The rolla stood there, frozen in his tracks.

"Li Chen, what just happened?"

"Voodoo! Rollas have very small souls, and because of this, they are very easy to control."

"Why didn't you stop him before?"

"Little soul, little voodoo. The voodoo will not last long."

Even as Li Chen was explaining this, the rolla began to move again. The rolla stood tall like a man, measuring in at roughly ten feet tall, likely weighing a ton or two. It turned its head toward us. The voodoo was quickly wearing off.

"We need to do something." Looking around for an idea, I noticed on the other side of the road, there was a large cliff that had a drop that was likely a half-mile deep. It was perfect, so I pointed to it and said to Li Chen, "We need to get him to roll off that cliff. I will get his attention and lure him close to the edge."

As the big stone man was regaining his senses, Li Chen and I made our way across the road to the edge of the cliff. I looked over the edge at the ground below and saw plenty of large boulders and rocks. The rolla continued to follow our movements with his gaze and began to head our way. In less than a second, it had transformed back into a sphere and was rolling straight toward us at maximum speed. Just before he reached us, we jumped out of the way and watched the massive being as it hurdled itself over the side of the cliff. The rolla was roughly thirty feet out into the air and falling fast before he hit the first jagged edge of the side of the cliff. A large piece of the stone man shattered off. He opened back up into the form of a man and looked like a broken, limp doll falling to its destruction. The rolla continued to hit rocky edge after edge until he finally hit the bottom in a thousand pieces. As the dust settled, we could see the pieces of the rolla resting with the other boulders at the bottom, almost as if they always belonged there.

Some of the other people came and peeked over the edge of the cliff to see the shattered rocks and leftover pieces of the rolla below. A crowd began to gather, and we could hear murmurs such as "What was that?"

Trying to think of a realistic answer, I said, "It must have been a boulder that came loose from the ridge up there." I pointed up the mountain as I said it, giving more life to my story.

Li Chen agreed with me, knowing he couldn't tell the crowd the truth. "Yeah, I saw it coming when it started rolling toward your cars."

"My insurance isn't going to believe this," said one of the bystanders.

Li Chen and I made our way back to the Mercedes and pulled back onto the highway and started following the *tick tick tick* of the crystal again. "We got really lucky back there," said Li Chen. "The rollas don't usually miss their targets. We must be getting close. The rolla hadn't been out of the book very long based on what we saw when we drove up. If it had been out of the book longer, there would have been a lot more carnage when we arrived."

We then drove in silence until my stomach started to rumble.

"Li Chen, what would you like to eat? Or . . . do you eat?" "Yes, I do eat, and some rice and honey would be good." "Well, that's just fine because I am famished and I feel like I could eat a horse—figuratively speaking. Let's see what we can find to eat."

Soon, we pulled off at the Cottage Grove exit on I-5. We saw a Denny's and decided to eat there, so we pulled into the parking lot. Li

Chen had the rice with some honey that he had wanted, and I had the Bob's Big Dog sandwich with onion rings, Diet Coke, and some pie. At first, Li Chen was drawing some curious eyes until they saw what I had to eat, and then we looked more like Denny's regulars. There was some small talk, mostly about the rollas. "Were there a lot of those creatures in the book? Where did they come from?"

Li Chen explained that there were at least twenty that he knew of in the book and that they came from Greece. "Rumor had it that the gods created them for a sport. It was a chess game of sorts. The rollas had a game of their own, and well, the chess game the gods were looking for was unruly at best. So the gods let them go, and that is how we have the ruins of Greece. The rollas were trying to play their games when Wilford Giloc placed them in the book at the request of the people of Greece. The rollas are very destructive, but in the book, they just play their games without the worry of destroying cities. Most of the inhabitants of the book enjoy the games on the weekends."

"On the weekends?"

"Yes, we try to maintain some sort of symmetry to reality. You know, such as what year it is when someone's birthday or anniversary is. Now not all are aware of their consciousness and choose not to live in the moment for food or love and hate or even the colors and textures that surround them in the book. Almost all are okay and have made peace with being there, but there are some that hate the book. Those people are the ones who would destroy everything. They would choose to try to rule the universe. And most of the time, they stay contained in the pages of the book."

Li Chen spoke as if he missed being in the book as if it were a place that even someone like myself wouldn't mind living in. It sounded like it is full of adventure, beauty, hope, happiness, mortality, maybe a friend or two, and grandeur. My life, so far, had been pretty confined to school and learning the old ways of magic and incantations from books and my parents. Now that they were gone, I had buried myself in my studies. I had become a shadow in society. Finding the book was becoming more than just a job; it had become my purpose for living, but I needed to stay focused on the job and not lose myself in what could be.

I-5 stretched a long way. Where could the thief possibly be going? Clearly, there was a specific destination. My feeling was that it was the Emerald City—Seattle, Washington. I didn't know why. Perhaps call it a hunch. We passed Eugene and then continued on to pass Salem, Oregon. The slow tapping of the crystal began to grind on my nerves, but at the same time, the slow and methodical tapping eased my mind as at least I knew I was on the right course. Li Chen slept as the Mercedes continued to roll on its northern journey. The rain began to come down like a wet gray blanket. At the time, it also reminded me of a ghost, the way the mist began to rise. I couldn't tell where the rain began or where the road met it; it was just a never-ending stream of gray with the occasional peek at the forest we were passing through and its dark green silhouette. Li Chen began to snore as loud as a chainsaw. My eyes were bloodshot. We needed real rest and soon. The gas tank was low on fuel, so I made the decision to stop in Kalana, Washington, for both rest and fuel. Between the driving and the rolla, the pounding rain made it easy to sleep with its constant rhythm lulling me into a deep, uninterrupted bliss.

We soon awoke to songbirds and sunshine, and I saw that Li Chen was sitting there, taking it all in. "We, of the book, sometimes forget the outside world that we are hidden from. It is so beautiful here. It makes me think of my home in China. I remember it so vividly, even after so many lifetimes away from it. I even remember the islands, when I was a voodoo slave. The blue water of the Caribbean, the solace of the jungles where I learned to love magic and its immortality. The dark gifts the magic could provide, absolute power over space and flesh, others' will at the mercy of your own. It was much like commanding a puppet on strings, so easy and intoxicating. Soon, the power and magic was overwhelming, and I became obsessed with my powers and having control. My soul began to wither and slip into another darker plane of existence, where I could not and would not retrieve it. The beauty around me darkened as well as the good in me began to fade. The book allowed me a chance at redemption. Wilford Giloc saved my life from the dark trances I was in." Li Chen paused, looking like he was coming back to the present. "So much for my bombastic interlude of memories.

I desire rum now. My breakfast can wait. You know, Sterling, we could just have rum for breakfast. That way, we could skip lunch altogether." Then Li Chen laughed a little and shook his head. "Rum for breakfast." We then both laughed.

It must have been eight in the morning when the blue light shimmered from my eyes again. I must have been in some sort of semitrance state; the vision was coming in loud and clear. There was the thief on a motorcycle; the knapsack was in plain view. My eyes started to look for anything that may give us some kind of clue as to where exactly the thief and the book were. It was at a 7-Eleven, and he was at the gas pump, fueling. The vision began focusing in on the bike. I was trying to scan the area for details, such as street signs, addresses, and land markers of any kind. It was of no use as the blue glare around the vision was too much. My eyes began to feel like they were starting to bleed, but I kept looking—up, down, and side to side. Then there it was, a sign—"Centralia, Washington, Population 15,000, City of Celebration. Come to Join Us!" The vision had stopped, and I immediately grabbed my eyes and held them for a few minutes.

"Are you all right?" asked Li Chen.

"Yes," I replied. "Get the map out of the glove box."

"The glove box?" he asked with a dumbfounded tone.

I pointed to it, and he fumbled a moment and then handed me the map. By this time, my sight was returning. Everything was still a white blur, but slowly, it came back. I flipped through the map till Washington State appeared. There it was, Centralia, and we were about fifty miles behind the thief if the vision was correct.

"We have about enough fuel. Let's head to Centralia. We can fuel there, and we will be that much closer to our prey," I said as I eyed my fuel gauge, seeing that the Mercedes was down to under a fourth of a tank. Nevertheless, the Mercedes was still running in top form as we rolled back onto the highway.

The sun was out, and it looked like a start to a beautiful day. Li Chen stared out of the window. He looked meek and white around the gills. "What is it, Li Chen?"

"I feel weak. I am beginning to fade. The vision and the time out of the book are taking a toll." He had been out of the book for a couple of days.

"How much time do you think you have left?"

"Don't know, but soon, I will have to return unto whence I came."

The Mercedes moved along the road as if it were riding on a feather nailed to the ground by the wind. It had already had a great ride to it. Forty-five minutes and we were at the sign that said Centralia. As we exited off the ramp, there was a 7-Eleven with a big sign that read, "City of Celebration. Come to Join Us!" There was no biker, but we were at the same pump. We fueled the car and used the rest of the money to grab four more cans of Red Bull. I thought it might pep Li Chen up. I know I was due for some. We grabbed two sandwiches from the cooler and a large bag of crunchy Cheetos, my favorites, as we pulled back onto the road. Li Chen was eating his hoagie and drinking a Red Bull.

After taking a huge gulp of the Red Bull, Li Chen held up the can and said, "This wine, it isn't bad!"

I laughed and smiled. "No, not bad at all." I sped the Mercedes up to 70 mph. "How do you think Mortrok is doing?"

"Well, he's had a couple of days in the book, so he should be doing just fine."

"Do you think I will ever see him again?"

"By all the gods, I think you shall, Sterling."

PURPLE ESSENCE

THE DAY WAS growing long, and Li Chen had talked most of it. The Red Bull was doing its job. He talked of China, the Caribbean, his world travels, and the book. He spoke of how Mortrok was his close friend, and he also talked of the purple essence of Queen Esmeralda. "Wherever she went, there was a purple mist that followed. She was so radiant that her essence leaked out of her in the form of that purple mist. Her essence could fill the room, and when you inhaled it, her essence would fill your heart with joy, and your soul would erupt like a volcano of happiness. The feeling of joy that the essence of Esmeralda brought to life, it was utopia, and it was intoxicating. Once her essence was in your lungs, blood, mind, and body, she can choose to take complete control. She has that kind of power over you, and that, Sterling, is a great power. When she chooses to take control, she can see as you see, sense where you have been, feel as you feel, and she can see what secrets lie beneath. All that is within us is now hers, and since she is queen, she can heal your pain or crush you with it. She is coming, Sterling. My powers are weakening, and thus, I must return to the book soon. The purpose for which I came is coming to an end. Look into yourself for the answers which you seek. They were put there a long time ago from your parents and from their parents' parents. You have been chosen. Your deductions will allow your conclusion to be absolute, and that is what it will take to save the book. Guard yourself, but always keep your mind's eye open, even in your dreams."

Li Chen's time with me was ending shortly as we continued toward the Polar North. Li Chen began to fade from the car seat until finally, he was nothing more than a slight vapor disappearing out the window. I slowed the Mercedes and pulled to the side of the road with hazards flashing and the crystal still tapping on the window shield. He was gone. Somehow in such a short period, greatness had come and gone twice in my life—the great Gen. Li Chen and Maury. My life had been forever changed. It was my life mission not only to find the book but also to recapture those whom I have known from this book.

At that moment, a new vision was forming. The blue glare from my eyes lit up the interior of the car. The thief was also on the side of the road, looking inside the backpack. Purple color was radiating out of it. Cars were passing at high rates of speed. He was on the side of the freeway with a large hillside to the right. There were little buildings on the side of the hill, cabin perhaps. The light on the hill would suggest the thief and I were in the same time zone. I began thinking that there must be more than what I was seeing, that I was missing something in this vision. Then there it was. As I adjusted the view of the vision, there was a large ship on a wide river or bay of some kind. These were clues I would have to watch for in the upcoming miles of my journey. The vision was gone just as fast as it had come. Without Li Chen, I was not sure I would have the vision, but that just made me more determined to find the book. Something also told me the purple glare from within the backpack was going to be a force to be reckoned with.

As the Mercedes rolled up I-5, everything was a little shaky. With too much Red Bull, it was getting hard to tell reality from dreams. Twenty minutes later, there was indeed a large ship floating in a wide river, and there were little toadstool cabins on the mountainside, just like in my vision. There was a resort of some kind not too far behind the hill.

My mind began running a little wild with the thoughts and plans of stopping the thief and obtaining the book. I began to run through a mental list of the tools I had with me to help me accomplish this mission—rope, holy water, flares, and my gun. I hesitated when I thought of my gun; I had not fired it in a year. If the thief was one of the mystical characters from the book, could they even be harmed by normal weapons like a gun? I just wasn't sure. I was able to deduce that the thief was capable and dangerous by evaluating their actions. The thief had enough fortitude to sneak into the monastery, open a century-old tree, and make off with the book I sought. The thief also managed to make it this far without destroying the world as we know it with the book's powers. This thief was going to be a formidable enemy.

As I drove on, I could not stop thinking about what Li Chen had said about Esmeralda. He had said that her purple essence was intoxicating, and in the vision, he had seen purple mist spilling out of the backpack the thief wore. Was this a sign that Esmeralda was trying to make her way out of the book? I was pulled out of my thoughts by a sharp tapping; the crystal was hitting the windshield with a force I had never seen before. The book must be here, but where? I had not seen anything around that indicated that the book was so close. I pulled the Mercedes to the gravel on the side of the road. All I could see was the dark forest to my right and the endless expanse of I-5 to my left. Cars flew by as rush hour began. I flipped the key on the grand old car to turn it off as it rumbled to a quiet stop. What was I missing? The crystal was now pegged to the windshield, but I still couldn't see anything. Then suddenly, a roaring flash of light appeared over the hood of my car. It was the bike. The bike then hit the ground, and the tires threw rock and sand at my windshield. The crystal released and began tapping quickly again. I turned the key to turn my car back on, and I hit the gas pedal as hard as I could. The chase was on.

As I pulled back onto I-5, the traffic was now heavy. The bike was already a quarter of a mile ahead of me as I made my way through the traffic. Suddenly, the inside of the Mercedes began to fill with smoke, purple smoke. The smoke was so thick that I had to roll the windows down so that I could drive. That was when I saw her sitting beside me, Esmeralda. She looked like the most beautiful woman I had ever seen. The purple mist that had surrounded her and filled my car was beginning to affect me. The mist filled my lungs, my mind, my heart, and my soul. I had to shake my head to clear my mind enough to look up at where I was driving. All I could see was the back end of a bus, and we were approaching fast, too fast. I hit my brakes and swerved, barely missing the bus. Then I heard her voice. Her voice was smooth like velvet and so soothing, euphoric almost. I instantly wanted to hear her speak more as she said, "Be careful, Sterling. Please concentrate on your driving." It took all my willpower to turn my focus back to the road. She spoke again, "You are more handsome than Mortrok or Li Chen gave you credit for, Sterling. But we must focus. We are close to the book."

"Book . . . what book?"

"The book of *Some Pictures*, Sterling. You must focus. We are all depending on you. If you could, please also roll down the windows to let some of the purple mist out of the car." I did as she asked.

My heart was beating rapidly, and my mind was reeling as I asked, "You . . . you are Esmeralda?"

"Yes, of course, but you already knew this."

"I did, and may I say that you are more beautiful than Maury and Li Chen described you?" She turned away as if to hide her blushing.

"Thank you, Sterling, but we really must stay focused on the task at hand—the book. We are very close."

The crystal tapped its familiar song against the windshield as the Mercedes rolled north on what seemed like an endless expanse of I-5.

"Are Mortrok and Li Chen all right? I mean, are they safe?"

"Yes," Esmeralda answered, "they are fine. They are safe in the pages of the book. They are safer in there than we are going to be out here as more and more evil are released into this world. Perkio and the drogs are rather tame in comparison with what we could eventually be facing. This is why you must catch the thief, Sterling! You must catch him soon, or we will all die." As Esmeralda spoke, the bike came back into view.

"There," I said. "Look just ahead. The thief and the book are close." "Yes, I see them, Sterling."

I pressed the accelerator down just enough to match the bike's speed. What should I do now though? I could ram the bike and shove it off the road, but then I ran the risk of exposing more of the magic and evil residing in the book to the world. Doing so could also possibly injure or kill the driver. I considered the option a little more, but the Mercedes was traveling at 70 mph, and any collision at that speed would be devastating. As I maneuvered the Mercedes closer to the bike, I turned to Esmeralda to try and ask what she thought we should do, but she was nowhere to be found. So as to avoid causing an accident, I turned my attention back to the motorcycle and the thief, only to see Esmeralda in front of and hovering above the bike. I had to slightly avert my gaze as the mist that surrounded her was bright, incredibly bright. She threw her arms apart, and the blinding glare caught the unsuspecting thief off guard. The bike swerved hard to the right, and the biker tried to dash under the purple glare, but Esmeralda had already adjusted her speed to match the bike. The thief tried to maneuver the bike to the right even more, but it was to no avail. The thief hit the brakes so hard that the back tire spun out and started to slide sideways across the ground. Esmeralda overcorrected and went too far to the right. Pressing the gas on the old Mercedes, the car pulled alongside the bike just as he hit the gas again. The bike lurched forward but not before getting caught by the Mercedes bumper, sending it into the air and then landing on the side of the road. The bike flipped over and over, causing dust, dirt, and rock to fill the air as the body of the rider slammed around as if it were a child's ragdoll, arms, legs, head over heels like it was being filmed in slow motion. The bike stood on its wheels for a final moment, almost to say "This is your last chance. You better get on." The motionless body did not obey, and the bike wobbled for the last time before falling to the ground. Pulling the Mercedes off the road just ahead of the lifeless body, I went running from the car to the thief's body. Esmeralda was already there, kneeling, searching the satchel for the book.

"Is he dead?"

"He is a she, and no, she is not dead. There is no book, Sterling. It must have fallen out of the bag. Help me look for it," Esmeralda said without concern for the thief.

"Forget the book. We have to make sure the girl is okay."

"Please, Sterling, if the book is open, then evil can escape."

"Okay," I said, not wanting to face more rollas. Besides, the rider looked like she was coming around, but still, something may have been broken.

Looking around toward the road and back to the side of the road, I did not see the book. The thief had rolled for at least twenty yards. Moving off the side of the road, in a bush, I saw a small light was shimmering. I began to have a sickening feeling in the pit of my stomach. Cautiously, I picked the book, and it was open. Not looking was not an option. I stared in wonderment as the page was alive with movement and all the color, a window into an alternate world, like a 3-D TV set, that was alive.

Esmeralda grabbed the book from my hand. "Sterling, do not stare. We must contain the book. Nothing must escape. I feel as though something may have already been released."

As she spoke, there was a sharp pain in the side of my skull, and everything was black. I was not sure how long I was out but not long after I hit the ground. Instincts, I suppose, caused me to move forward as I felt the glancing blow. This time I was able to roll sideways and caught myself. It was the rider. She moved in again with a front kick that landed in my chest and knocked me over on my butt and then a front roll kick that I managed to roll away from as she landed on her butt. Throwing a rolling right kick, I caught her flush in the jaw. Momentarily stunned, I jumped to my feet and tried to fill my lungs with air again. The thief sat there dazed and swaying back and forth. Picking her off the ground, I placed her in an armlock known as a hammerlock.

Esmeralda stood a few feet away, saying, "Well, now that was • • __ " impressive.

"All right, kid, who are you, and who sent you to steal the book?" I asked.

"Screw you, bald man!" the thief screamed.

"That was not very respectful," I said as I tightened the hammer lockup between her shoulder and back.

"You're breaking my arm!"

"Start talking, or you will be able to scratch your head from the back."

"Okay, okay, my name is Tara Jones." I squeezed a little harder. "I work for some private individuals out of Seattle," she said.

"Come on, who are they, and where can I find them?" I said.

She moaned from the pain. "I don't know. I am supposed to call when I get there."

"Let her go, Sterling. We have the book," said Esmeralda.

"No, Esmeralda, if we do not find them, we may never make it back to St. Rayes." I turned my attention back to Tara. "All right, Tara, you are going to call them and tell them the bike is broken to get them to come down here and get the book. Do you think you can do that, or do I have to break more than your arm?" I asked as I twisted it a little tighter.

"Okay, okay, I will call. My phone is in my backpack. It has the number."

"Okay, let's get the bike out of the road, and no funny business, or I will shoot you."

We moved the bike to the side of the road. Tara Jones complained the whole way about what we have done to her bike.

"It's all scratched up. Not cool, old people!" she said with disdain and a bit of disrespect like we were the ones in the wrong here.

"All right, but the bike is not hurt that bad."

"Yeah, no, thanks to you," she said as she put the bike on its kickstand. Esmeralda handed Tara the backpack. She took it very awkwardly and asked if Esmeralda was from the book and then shook her head and said, "Of course, you are. How could you float and light up like that otherwise?" She then turned to face me and said, "And who are you?

"I am Sterling Gray. I was hired to retrieve the book you stole," I said.

"Stole? I didn't steal anything. I was hired to deliver the book to Seattle."

"Who hired you to deliver it?"

"Some old dude. He was a little older than you. He said he would give me $2,000 if I could get there by tomorrow. He gave me one thousand up front and promised the second payment of one thousand when I get the book there. He gave me the backpack and the money and said there was a phone inside the backpack. I was told to hit redial on the phone when I got to Seattle and not to open the book or the backpack until then."

"But you didn't do that, did you?"

"No, I didn't, and I have been running like hell ever since. That book is possessed by a lot of evil spirits. Like her and the China man and his blue devil dogs from hell."

Checking to see how real her story was, I searched for her ID and found she had about nine hundred in cash on her. The sky began forming some very dark and ominous clouds. As Tara kept checking out her bike, the wind began to blow much harder, causing the dust to whip through the air like sandpaper without the paper. Fumbling through the satchel, while partially trying to cover my face from all the wind and dust, I could hear as the bike roared to life. Tara was off in a streak of darkness.

I began to chase after her when Esmeralda said, "Sterling, we have to return the book to St. Rayes."

The storm grew stronger with full-force winds. "Okay, Esmeralda, let's get in the car," I said as the torrential rain began to fall.

We made it to the car. As it rocked back and forth from the winds, Esmeralda said, "Get back on I-5, head to the first exit, and then head south." With the book in hand, she said, "I think something may have been released back there."

"What was it, King Neptune? I have never seen rain like this before. What about Tara? I do not think this is the last we will see of her."

The Mercedes rumbled south through the bad weather. It seemed to have been following us. The crystal was no longer tapping; it was just pointing at the book that had tiny pinholes of light glaring from it.

"A tempest spirit has escaped from the book. The only one I know is Kindra, and if it is her, we are going to need help. As far as I know, she is the storms from the seas or at least part of her." Lightning was striking all around the car, with the wind pushing hard on the car. We felt ourselves go airborne. "Hopefully, Kindra will release us from her storm. She is part storm and part dragon. She is furious and unrelenting. She may not know we have the book yet and may still think Tara still has it. In any case, we need to get out of here fast and not look back. We must outrun the storm as she may lose her power over the storm, so after that, Kindra the black dragon will not relent."

Esmeralda threw her hands in the air and began to say an old incantation in an ancient language, perhaps Egyptian or Sumerian, but whatever it was, it started to work. A large purple fog bank appeared, and the Mercedes entered into the still purple mist. There, the wind and rain ceased. We were surrounded by the purple mist with just the straight white line of the highway before us. The speedometer indicated we were traveling about 75 mph, but it felt as if we were going 20. Out of the corner of my eye, I caught a flickering glimpse of a black streak. It was Tara on her bike, passing in the mist. She must have been following us in the storm. The bike charged forward, almost out of control, into the mist and then out of sight.

"This is only temporary, Sterling," said Esmeralda.

She was tiring, and I pushed the pedal down to the floor. We exited the mist, and Esmeralda fainted. As quickly as we had entered the mist, we were out again. The review mirror suggested the storm was miles behind us.

"Esmeralda? Esmeralda!" I screamed her name, trying to awaken her.

She gleamed a little and then opened her eyes as she said, "Sterling, I have to get back in the book."

"It's too soon," I said. Her presence was needed here. She needed to stay here with me. If she went back into the book, how could I breathe, how could I see? Everything without her would be dull. There would be no color, no life, and only my sorrow would exist. "Not yet, Esmeralda, not yet," I said.

"No, not yet but soon, Sterling," she replied.

Not wanting to think past the inevitability that she would have to go back at some point, I focused my attention back on the road and my car. I then noticed the car was traveling at 80 mph and made a mental note to slow down. That kind of speed could not be good for the car or for us. So being more mindful of our speed, we moved through the night safe and unnoticed, but I could not help but feel that Tara was out there close by us and that Kindra was going to be on our tails soon. Esmeralda rested, and her breathing was beginning to labor. Two hours had passed, and my adrenaline was waning. Heck, who was I kidding?

I was just plain tired and needed a serious pickup. Our journey was at hand, so the first rest stop with vending machines would have to do.

In and out, keep moving; we were racing time, darkness, and evil, all the while preserving the precious remaining time with Esmeralda. I loved her from the moment I saw her. Since the purple mist had filled my eyes, I began loving her. I thought, *Surely this must be that way it is with all who know her.* We had traveled for hours and were now down near Kelso, Washington. The Mercedes needed gas, and I needed to rest, but that wasn't going to happen. I saw exit 36. There was a shell station, just what the doctor ordered. Esmeralda was asleep, so I picked up some fruit and salad for her as well as a Red Bull, Cheetos, and Slim Jims for myself. I fueled the car, checked the water and the oil, and was in and out of that gas station like NASCAR. I felt someone was watching, and that made the hair on my neck stand on end.

As the tires began to roll on the I-5 South, the Red Bull began to kick in. Esmeralda was still sleeping. I had not the heart to wake her. She gleamed in beauty, and all I could do was look to fill my heart with her. She was beginning to fade back to the book and fade from me to the pages of her home and, at that moment, my hell. Simply, I loved her. About an hour had passed when she woke from her slumber.

"How was your nap?" She responded with a yawn that was huge and befitting of a queen.

"You should have wakened me. There is much you need to know about the book. First, you need to get it back to St. Rayes and the Brothers of the Suffering Order. Sterling, there is great power in the book, and there already may be sorcerers, witches, and evil that are like Kindra the black dragon that may also be from the book. As you also know, none of us can survive more than a few days outside of the book unless we can control the book."

"What about you? Tell me about you. What are you?"

"There is no time for that, Sterling. I am fading as you can see, but it is all in here, in the book, as you will see."

There were a loud thud and a sickening crunch on the front of the Mercedes. It was Tara Jones. Her bike had roared off the hood of the car as she unloaded multiple shots into the car.

"Esmeralda, my gun is in the glove box! Hand it to me!" I said while rolling down the window to get a clean shot of my own. Tara was at least fifty to sixty yards ahead of us. Steadying my hand on the door between the mirror and the frame, I got off two shots.

One must have missed the bike, and the other ricocheted, and then she was gone into the night. I turned to Esmeralda to check to see if she was all right. She appeared to be fine, and I pulled over the Mercedes to assess the damage. The hood was bent like a pair of bat wings, along with a bullet hole in the corner of the windshield on Esmeralda's side, and the grill was missing from the radiator. We were very lucky, I thought, as I got back into the car and found Esmeralda nearly transparent.

She spoke very softly, "I was in Caracas many years ago, blessed by a good savior who believed in my beauty and that I should reign as queen, which was not my wish, but it was my duty. It was greater than me that the good should be done. Sorry, Sterling, I must leave you for now."

I leaned in to kiss her. She was gone, and she had faded back into her home in the book. She went back to her friends and her family and the safety of her book, which now must be guarded with my life. They all must endure and continue to thrive within the book's pages, not just for their sake but also for mine.

This book, with all its love, honor, compassion, and friendship, was the only real compassion I had known since my parents had died.

THE DARK STORM

THE SKY OVER Portland, Oregon, was black with rain, wind, and lightning. There was continuous turbulence, and chaos was unseen in these skies. The weather report suggested just a bad cell passing through these parts as so many had passed through the Oregon coastline. It was, in fact, famous for its torrential rainfall. So people went about their day in their normal manner, rushing under a ledge way or a building canopy, adjusting their umbrellas as they moved across the windswept streets, unaware of the wind that was drenching Anorak Cagoule raincoats or the raindrops that were ever so softly upward and landing on their faces like a quenched landscape with morning dew. Tonight's meal consumed their thoughts. A partner's engagement at the morning breakfast table, about being home as early as possible, their favorite song and dance show on at eight were what was going through their minds.

I knew better. It was Kindra the black dragon searching for the book and was not that far behind. I pushed the pedal down, and the Mercedes picked up speed. I had to stay ahead of the storm. Because of her winds, the power lines were down all over Portland. As she tore through the city, the water trapped many cars. As Kindra became more and more agitated, lightning and thunder flashed like strobe lights in a nightclub and the booming sound like the DJ's speakers. All this time, I was thinking Tara Jones was somewhere out there with her pistol scope on me, not at all thinking what other evil or magic could be coming from the book. The dark storm increased in velocity, and I could see its ravages in the rearview window mirror with its blackness and flashes of lightning.

Now the Mercedes was traveling at 75 mph. How did it know the book was headed south? I envisioned the black dragon intertwined with the sky.

"Every time the hood of my car comes into sight, it angers me! Tara was going to have to pay for that and the bullet holes," I said to myself.

A bright light appeared ahead, so illuminating one had to notice. I slowed the car, and there were two people, a young man and young woman, dressed in all white with light skin and blond hair. They held their right hands up to wave. The Mercedes came to a stop just past the two. They opened the car door, and at first, I had to cover my eyes as they requested to please enter the car.

"I am in a hurry," I replied. The girl was first, but the Mercedes did not really have a back seat. She made her way in between the seat and found a place to rest. The young man then got in and shut the door. "Sterling Gray is my name."

"We know, Sterling. Esmeralda and Mortrok told us," they replied.

"So you are from the book!"

"Yes, we are illumina. This is my sister, Shimmer, and I am Sunny. We are here to help with the dark storm any way we can. Kindra is very powerful as you can already see. She can turn day into night with her darkness. Her storm could cover a whole city. The three of us may be able to defeat her fury. Your ability to see and adapt to magic is going to be the key to holding her back until she must return to the book. We must try to contain her in a small space. As long as she is able to spread out, her storm can come with the full strength. That could very well stop us. The black dragon is very powerful, smart, and cunning to say the least. Her environment and light are her weaknesses. That is why illumina are needed to fight her. We illumina are children of the sun. The sun provides the power, which is needed to defeat her," Sunny said.

The car returned to I-5 South. Sunny spoke of small places along the way, where the storm may be contained such as canyons, tunnels, and large structures like buildings, someplace where she would not be able to blow the walls down. Shimmer told of how everyone in the book was pulling for me, at least those who were not evil. She went on to describe how there was no evil in the book until they escaped from the book's confinement. Then and only then, they would regain control of the evil power if they so desired. At one time, most all people in the book desired power or the dark side, but the book can, and did, change most. The effects of the book were beginning to take a toll on me; Esmeralda's love spell, Mortrok's magic, Li Chen's visions, and now the illumina were all taking something from me—small pieces, slices—or even tearing from me as a whole, pieces of my mind, my soul, and my heart. It didn't feel bad but just not like me. The Mercedes rolled on as the beautiful view became a blur. It was getting harder and harder to concentrate. It was time for a break. We left I-5 at exit 200 in Springfield, Oregon. Just off the ramp was BP station with around twenty pumps. I found the farthest pump from the store as to not draw unwanted attention to the illumina twins.

"Do you have to use the bathroom?" I asked.

"No, but some snacks would be great," they replied.

I should have known that was what they would have wanted. They were teenagers after all. We went inside the store, and I advised them to get what they wanted since I had to use the potty. They both giggled at my use of the word "potty."

"We are over four hundred years old. It is funny you go potty," they said as they turned their attention to the contents of the store.

As I washed my hands and face, I could not shake the feeling I was in danger. The twins had loaded the counter with junk food and two cans of Red Bull and Cheetos for me. The total came to $53.64 after fuel.

"We don't get these snacks in the book. In fact, it is the same old foods day in and day out. Yes, we must change this."

They laughed like giddy school children. It made me feel warm inside, and all of this was worth it. That warm feeling did not last long. As we began to get on the freeway, that old feeling of danger returned. Scouring our vicinity, nothing appeared to set off alarms. However, the feeling was strong. Tara Jones was near, and this made me feel more on edge. I felt more responsible for the young people in my car with me. Tara must not hurt us.

"Sterling, may we call you Sterling?" asked Shimmer.

"Yes, you may," I replied to her.

"Wasn't sure you see Mortrok. He kept telling your story," they said with big eyes and smiles. "Li Chen said you are much more powerful than you think and that he admired you immensely. Your knowledge of magic was only superseded by your inherent deductive powers, a high compliment from a man with great magical powers of his own."

Shimmer started to sing "Voodoo Like You Do." She and Sunny started to laugh a big belly laugh. "Li Chen is our very good friend. He and Mortrok are almost like fathers to us. Yes, I would say they are our much-beloved family."

The car was rolling smoothly in the southern direction. I popped the top of a Red Bull, drinking it in one big gulp, followed by a bigger burp. "Excuse me, not bad manners, just good stuff."

We all laughed, and the twins followed suit with their bottles of soda. It was truly like we were family, just out for a ride in the family car. The twins spoke of times when they would leave the book to enjoy life's little pleasures, such as soda, arcades, and other young people.

We passed the mountains with great green canopies and jagged rock and waterfalls. Blue skies and black ribbons of the road held the car down on it southern path. We reached the Northern California border. The lights, as well as the fuel, were running low. A stop was needed. The rest was also needed. I could not help but wonder if Kindra or Tara needed rest or fuel. I didn't know, but I had to keep pushing onward. We pulled in for the night to a preppy little town with shops lined with Mayan emblems as a tourist attraction. Being in the car for so many days, I could not afford the room in the car to sleep. Motel 6 looked darn good. Going into the office, I booked one room with two queens and a cot. We made our way to the room. Sunny spoke up and said he would take the cot.

With the book secure in my suitcase, I gave the kids $20 to order a pizza. I let the kids know I was going to take a shower. In the restroom, I looked into my eyes. They were bloodshot, and looking back was a man in his late 30s going on 60. What had I accomplished? Letting the family business go by the wayside, a degree that was not worth much, and magic that was sporadic at best. After the hot shower and the new clothes, I felt like a new man.

There was a knock at the door. "Pizza!" exclaimed Sunny as he ran to the door. He went to open it just as the door was kicked in, the edge of the door catching him square on the chin. Sunny landed six feet away, flat on his back. I looked at the doorway, wondering who had kicked the door in. It was Tara Jones. I dove for my suitcase where my gun was lying, but Tara had already gotten the drop on us.

"Do not move, everyone, or it will be your last!" Tara said. "Get down on the floor, all of you! Do it now! All right, Mr. Gray, where is it?"

"It is in my suitcase," I said.

"Smart choice, Mr. Gray, because my next move was to put a hole in your kneecap." Tara closed the door behind her and slowly made her way to the suitcase. She fumbled a bit and pulled out my .38 and said, "I'll be taking that!" She then stuffed the gun in her waistband. She began to toss items out of the suitcase until she had retrieved the book. Tara then began backing out of the door, when a huge gust of wind blew her clear across the room into the doorframe of the bathroom, and she was out colder than a mackerel.

What I saw next blew my mind. A large dragon head attached to about six feet of neck appeared before us. It was ferocious and violent. The large head swayed back and forth, snapping its formidable teeth. The eyes were the shape of footballs and flaming red. What came next astounded me. Shimmer became molten white and began to transform into a four-foot-long saber. Sunny dove toward the saber. Sunny began to grow three feet taller and two feet wider and now bore a shield, a helmet, and a breastplate that shone as bright as the sun. I was momentarily blinded by the light, and partially covering my eyes, I was able to see the battle begin. Sunny began to slash at the dragon with the saber. The dragon snapped wildly with its razor-sharp teeth. The dragon's body would not fit through the door, but its huge head and neck were pushing further into the room. Seeing a mist from Shimmer and Sunny, the dragon snapped again and again. Sunny ducked and rolled to the door, and with one mighty thrust, the saber went into the heart of the dragon. It threw its head back as the light began to burst through its skin, but with one last great snap, it grabbed Sunny by the head and torso. In defeat, the dragon had won the battle. They all were gone. A slight glimmer of light was all that was left of Sunny. The dragon and Shimmer had disappeared in an instant. Tara Jones remained unconscious, and it was time to check out of the motel, but this time Tara was going with me. Tying her hands with her belt, I carried her to the car and tightly strapped her in with her hands behind her back. I packed up the Mercedes and hit I-5 South. There was no chance of sleeping now.

She was out cold with a pretty good knot on her head. At first, I thought perhaps take her to the hospital, but there was no time. Maybe I should just throw her out of the car. After all, she did try and kill me twice. She moaned a bit and rolled her head back and forth and then went back to sleep. It must have been a lot of money to her to be this daring. The heist itself must have taken extreme planning, cunning, and bravery, or maybe she was just a maniac gun for hire. Whatever it was, I had to be careful. I pulled the car to the side of the road in a screeching stop and went to the passenger side, where I began going through her leather jacket, books, and pants pockets. I recovered a .9 mm Beretta, a six-inch duck knife, and brass knuckles with spikes—every hit man's Christmas list. I put the hit man or, in this case, hit woman's gun in my overstuffed pockets.

About ten miles down the road, Tara Jones began to wake up. "What the fuck!" she exclaimed.

"Calm down. You are in my car, Tara."

"What the hell happened?"

"You found us in the Motel 6. The problem was Kindra the black dragon found you, and you led her to us. You kicked the door in, and when she arrived, she blasted you almost across to the other side of the room. A battle ensued, and everyone else died. Now you are with me, mostly for my safety," I replied.

TARA JONES

SLIGHT FRAME WITH dark hair and dark eyes, her hair was cropped short but not boyish. She was dressed in all black leather with lace-up boots. There was no makeup or perfume. Tara Jones overall was very cute and deadly. As we headed farther south into Northern California, she arranged herself into the seat to be more comfortable.

"So now what, Mr. Gray? Will you take me back to face justice and my accusers?

"Yeah, something like that. But it is a long ride still, so how about we talk?" I said.

"Sure, Mr. Gray. What would you like to talk about?"

"First, call me Sterling. Second, telling me who you are working for would be a good starting place."

"Okay, Sterling, as you know already, I work for some very powerful people in Seattle. So you know about as much as I do about that. Now it is your turn. Who do you work for? The brothers, I assume."

"That would be correct. My turn, who helped you get into St. Rayes?" I asked.

"Do you mean did I have an accomplice? No. Speaking of accomplices, where are the two light bulbs you were carrying around?" she asked with a snicker.

"Do you mean the two light bulbs that saved your bacon? They are gone back into the book, I hope. Their names were Shimmer and Sunny."

She laughed out loud. "Their names, I mean, don't you find that funny? You said they went back to the book? As in into the book? Man, you are out there. Dragons, people that light up like stars . . . Sterling,

I do not believe any of this story you are telling me. What are you on, drugs? Have you been drinking a lot, Sterling? It's just an old book, nothing more."

"Well, ask yourself this: if it is just an old book, why do your employers want it so bad? They hired a hit person to retrieve it."

"Easy. It is worth a lot of money. It is an antique. Some collectors want it for their lush library."

"Have you opened the book? You must have seen what came out of it. When you were riding in the storm, you must have known something was different. You must have seen things that weren't normal. No, I just do not believe you, Tara."

"You are crazy, Sterling. You should never pick up hitchhikers. That could be very bad for your health."

"You mean hitchhikers like you?"

"Yes, I mean, like me and all of the others you have allowed in your little fantasy."

I thought either she was a really good liar or she was so focused on me and the book that she hadn't seen the anomalies. Whatever the case was, I felt she was dangerous, and I would not be letting my guard down. In fact, this was probably the safest place for her and me, but I could not let the book fall into the hands of the authorities. No matter how far-fetched the story sounded, testing the legitimacy was not an option.

Tara spoke up, "I have to use the ladies' room."

Her statement sent shivers through me. "We can stop soon."

She repeated the statement again a few moments later. "I have to go to the restroom, Sterling."

"Okay," I replied and pulled up to a line of eucalyptus bushes on the side of the road, got out of the car, and went to release her seat belt. "If you try anything, I will shoot you. Do you understand?"

"You are going to have to untie my hands."

I replied, "I do not think so."

"Well, how am I supposed to do this?"

I thought for a moment and then gave in and untied her hands. "Just remember, no funny business, or I will shoot you. Turn around." She did. "You face that way, and I will turn this way."

I had always been brought up to respect ladies from an early age, but this was no lady. As soon as my back was turned, she hit me with a savage left hook, which made me see stars. After I turned around from the force of the punch, she hit me with a straight right hand to the bridge of the nose.

Even brighter stars, but I was not yet out of my head. Using her combat boots, she struck me right under the chin and lifted my body off the ground. I was out cold. The next few moments were black and then flashes of my body being dragged into the car, and then it was back to darkness.

As I came to, I realized I was now the one who was tied up. All I could do was think about how much of a dumbass I was. What the hell was I thinking? My mind immediately went to the book. Had she opened it to see if what I had said was true? It appeared like she had not so far.

Tara was exiting off I-5, and I thought she must be heading back to Seattle to deliver her goods to her employer. I thought it was best to pretend to sleep till I could get my chance to spring on her. This woman was clearly a dynamo who could and would fight, but why did she not leave me on the side of the road? She must have believed me some about the book and its magical powers. As she pulled the car onto the ramp for I-5 North, she pulled to the side of the road and put the car in park. As she did, she turned around and began shaking me awake while saying, "Wake up! Wake up!"

"I'm awake! So what is it going to be?"

"So let's say I believed you about the book," she said with an almost frightened tone.

"Well, the safest thing to do would be to take it back to where you stole it from."

"Then what?" she asked.

"Then you go your way, and I go my way," I finished.

"That sounds all good, but my employer is not going to let it drop that easy," she said.

"We will just have to hope the brothers at St. Rayes have an alternative plan for keeping the book safe." I paused and then asked, "Why the change of heart all of the sudden?"

"I am not sure, but it has become clear to me now that my employers wouldn't let me live with or without the book. And just for your information, I could have killed you a long time ago," Tara said with a sullen tone.

"Well, thanks for that," I mumbled. "I sure could have done without the ass-kicking you gave me back there."

"Oh, that was nothing. It's not like you haven't torn up my bike and tied me up. Now we are even."

"Where did you learn to fight like that?" I asked.

"I was MMA rank number 3 in the 105-pound class. My discipline is Muay Thai. I have other skills as well, such as jujitsu and judo. I am also a pistol and rifle expert. I learned from a badass marine sniper." She paused and smiled, seeming to reminisce. "I learned to ride bikes around the age of nine, but it was mostly for fun."

"You . . . having fun? You don't seem like the type to have fun!" I exclaimed.

"Now see, that is funny, Sterling. You are a funny guy. This partnership is going to work out just fine," she said as she smiled.

My head felt like it was still half full of cobwebs, and my eyeballs were still incredibly sore, which probably meant I had a concussion. Neurocognitve testing was definitely in order. "So here is the plan. I help you return the book, and you go to your employer, and I get $5,000. That is five times as much as I was getting paid, but with what all I have been through, it is not out of the question."

Tara Jones backed the Mercedes up the ramp and headed south on I-5. "Sterling, I want to see what is in the book. I want to see some of the magic that you keep talking about."

"No way! You have spilled more out of the book that was humanly safe. You honestly did not see the blue drogs?"

"Drogs! No, I have not seen anything." She swung the car to the side of the highway and slammed the Mercedes hard into park. "I want to see! Anything, something magic from the book!"

"First of all, I do not know how it works. Somehow something spills out, and you do not know if it is friend or foe, nice or mean," I said.

"That sounds like a lot of horseshit to me. Let me see the book."

"No way! I am telling you, Tara, bad, bad things come out of this book."

Tara pulled my .38 out and pointed it at me and said, "Open the frigging book."

"I could open it and an eight-foot rolla could be in the front seat with us." I stared at her, hoping she would change her mind. She didn't. I sighed resolutely and said, "Okay, you asked for it." I opened the book, closed my eyes, and flinched from the pain I had not felt yet. The next thing I heard made my heart skip a beat, and my worry subsided ever so slightly.

"Look at that, Sterling! Oh wow!" Slowly, I opened my eyes to see the most beautiful bouquet of sparkling flowers that looked as if they were growing out of the dash. As I closed the book, the sparkle began to fade and the blue radiating light began to dim. "Oh wow," she said again. "It's true. The book is magic."

"No, the book is very dangerous."

The flowers lay on the dash like a floral carpet with a very strong lavender smell. At that point, a vision hit me, throwing my head back into the seat. There was no reckoning of time or space; the lights were flashing blue, red, and green inside a purple circle, which, when looked through, appeared almost like a kaleidoscope. I felt like I was leaning into the future. I could see myself dragging Tara's lifeless body to cover. White-hot bolts of light were burning through tile and rocks. As best as I could tell, there were large buildings all around me, and it was late in the day. The vision stopped as abruptly as it came, but all I could remember was the white bolts of light and dragging Tara's lifeless body and the tall building in the woods.

"Welcome back, sleepyhead," Tara said jokingly. "Must have kicked you harder than I thought."

"How long was I out?" I asked.

"About forty-five minutes or so," she said.

"The visions put me in a voodoo trance. Compliments of my friend Li Chen."

"Your friend is hitting you with a voodoo trance?"

"No, he gave me the ability to have the visions, but they come and go when they want to. These are from someone in the book."

"What do you see in these visions?"

"Mostly the future."

"Do you mean like lotto numbers?"

"I don't know, mostly scenes. This last one was the woods with tall buildings and lightning flashes."

"Was I there?" Tara asked.

"Yes, you were there," I replied, gazing off in the distance to avoid eye contact.

"Wow, let's get to it!" she exclaimed as she pushed on the gas. "We would be heading into Redding, California, soon. We were going to have to call it a night there."

Something felt wrong, I thought. Maybe it was because I was concussed, or perhaps like I had been drugged. I had been traveling all day, driving from Weed, California, to Redding, California. The two cities were only 125 miles apart. Had Tara been driving in circles all day, stalling, waiting for her employer to show up? I had been unconscious for most of the day. What was going to happen was going to happen in Redding? I checked for my gun, but it was not on me. Tara must have it as well as hers. *Just play it cool,* I thought. My head was hurting, and I was going to need all my cognitive reasoning and physical strength to defeat Tara, even though somehow I wanted to believe in her.

What was it with the women on this case? I felt like I kept falling for them. Was it a residual effect of Esmeralda's love mist with it hypnotic feels inducing grandeurs of love? Could it be that I spent so much time in the mysteries of the Macabre and work in the paranormal, or was it that my life was just that boring and these women were that exciting? I was not sure, but I could not let these emotions interfere with my job. My life depended on it now more than ever.

It was just about dark when Tara pulled into the Econolodge just south of Redding. The sunlight was all gone, but a glimmer that concealed the orange building made it look dull. As the Mercedes came to a stop, the lodge's lights came on. They were illuminating the office where other patrons were securing a room for the night. They were weary travelers for I-5 and beyond. Tara took the keys and her knapsack with the book inside.

"Don't go anywhere now," she said as she smiled a devilish grin.

The deafness was gone now, but my jaw still hurt. I was interested to see how this was all going to play out. There was no need for me to retrieve the spare key located under the dash. She returned and said we were in room 19 on the bottom floor.

"Why, do you think I am too old for the second floor?"

She laughed. "I had not thought about that. Are you?" She laughed some more.

As we entered room 19, she threw the knapsack on the first bed, proclaiming this as hers like a kid calling shotgun in the car. Throwing my drained body on the other bed, I thought this would work just fine.

"Why don't you order us some pizza or something while I take a shower?" she said as she disappeared into the restroom with the knapsack that she was coveting.

As outrageous as this had all been, this somehow sounded good to me. I was still wondering if my gun was in the knapsack or on the side of the road, perhaps even in the Mercedes. I didn't know and could not think about that right now. I turned my attention to ordering the pizza. I ordered an extra large with all-meat pizza and a two liter of Pepsi. They said it would be about forty-five minutes as they were busy this time of the day. I hung up the phone and yelled, "Pizza is on the way!" There was no response, so I moved closer to the door to yell again. I received an okay that time. I proceeded to the mirror to examine myself. Both my cheeks looked swollen. As I rubbed my chin, hellish pain radiated through my body. It did not feel good getting my ass handed to me. I needed to go to bed after I showered and got some clean clothes and a good shave. As I waited my turn for the bathroom, I stared out the motel window. Everything looked okay, but I could not shake this feeling trouble was on its way.

A few moments later, she returned from the bathroom with her hair wet in just a sports bra and panties. She threw the knapsack on the bed and let me know it was my turn as she used the towel briskly to dry her hair. The bra was wet and barely covering her breasts. She had a lot of bruises, which caused me to feel sorry for her despite the pain still radiating from my chin. She was still very beautiful.

The mirror in the bathroom was steamed up as I took my hand across it to clean it off. I was going to shave and jump in the shower. The good thing about the motels is that they always have hot water. Standing there for a long time, just letting the water run across my body, felt very good. I was thinking about how I understood what had happened with Esmeralda with the magic and all, but this Tara Jones caused me to feel something different. I toweled off and dressed, putting on my pants. It was hot and steamy. I left the room without my shirt to cool off.

Tara was sitting there with both guns and the book in front of her. One of the guns was mine.

"You should put that book away," I said as I bent down to retrieve my gun. It was still loaded. "Now put the book away," I repeated.

"Sure, okay, I will put it away," she said as she slipped it into her knapsack.

About that time, there was a knock at the door. It was the pizza delivery. I paid the driver and set the pizza on the dresser. As I turned, Tara was standing very close to me. She said she was very hungry as she placed her arms around my neck, leaning up to kiss me. I pulled her in tight, inhaling her beauty with my eyes at first and then tenderly kissing her, and then the force of her passion overtook me as well. I lifted her in the air and carried her to the bed. We were only slowed down by the time it took for us to tear each other's clothes off. I placed my right hand onto the small of her back as she arched with pleasure. She was magnificently flexible, but as a former high school football player, I was no slouch either. Three and a half hours later, we collapsed into each other's arms.

It was somehow midnight by this point, and there was a knock at the door. We rolled out of bed in our underwear, fumbling to try to find our guns. Just as I located my .38, the door blasted open, splintering into a thousand pieces. Shots rang out from the door like machine-gun fire, possibly a Mach .10 machine pistol. I rolled over to the far bed and yelled for Tara to get down. I was able to squeeze out a couple of shots, and the first person went down as the second person came through like Superman, gun blasting. It was dark, but every time the gun went off, it gave me a silhouette to aim at. I was able to take the second gunman down with two shots to the head.

The room went quiet. "Tara, are you okay?" I said in as loud of a whisper as I could.

"Yes, I am fine," she replied.

Peering out the window, I was unable to see anyone else, but lights from the other rooms began to come on. We quickly got dressed, knowing we had to get out of here. The Mercedes was burning rubber in less than two minutes. When we were safely back on the road, I decided to ask "Your employer, I assume?"

"I used a fake name, paid with cash, and told them I was in a truck. Yet my employer still found us."

"Did you tell them at some point where you were?"

"Yes, but that was before you showed me the magic of the book and . . . well . . . before last night. Sterling, I am sorry!"

"Yes, I am sure you are!" I checked the mirrors. No one appeared to be following us. "Your little setup got two men killed and almost got us killed."

"Yes, I almost got us killed, all right? Now calm down. We are in the same boat here. They want you dead, and the only way out of this is if we work together to get this book back to the Brothers of the Suffering Order at St. Rayes. First, we need to take a detour. They will be looking for us along I-5."

"Look in the glove box. There is a map." She reached in the glove box and handed me the map I had mentioned. I peered at the map quickly while controlling the vehicle. "It looks like Highway 99 will be our best bet. They will be looking for us along I-5, and 99 will take us all the way down from Bakersfield. Highway 99 will be a little more rundown, but we are making good time. In Sacramento, we will gas up and grab some food," I said as we drove on.

The trip had become mostly quiet. We didn't talk much and barely made eye contact. We got the gas and some food, and then we were back on the road. Highway 99 had been the main road between Bakersfield and Sacramento for years before I-5 was built. Old factories, old homes, and farms lined the way. The broken, sunken slabs of concrete for miles there was a *clump, clump, clump* sound that the tires would make as we passed over the old road. There were eucalyptus trees flowering as they twisted together, forming a natural but weird frame along the road as we drove in silence for miles and miles.

Finally, I said, "Did you mean what you said earlier about us, Tara?"

Tara looked confused for a moment. "Yes, yes, of course, I did. You must have felt it too. I mean, between us, you felt it too . . . right?" she questioned me.

She was totally right. Damn, it was almost spiritual. "Yes, I felt it."

As I looked into her dark eyes, the sensation was real, and it was right. I pulled over to the side of the road into a wide spot. The emotions took over us as we joined together in each other's arms. The kisses were deep and meaningful, full of passion. We were very excited and needed more than a wide spot off the road would allow for. This would all have to wait; the book was the most important thing right now on our agenda for both of us. We pulled back from each other and got back on the road.

"I am going to need a new bike, Sterling. Is that going to be a problem?" she asked.

"No, why would it be?"

"Well, it is just that some men would be too intimidated."

"After getting my butt kicked, the bike seems kind of tame." We both laughed.

Not only was she easygoing, smart, and as tough as nails, but her beauty also reminded me of what Cleopatra must have looked like. I could not become overcome by her and had to stay focused on the job at hand. The Brothers of the Suffering Order and the inhabitants of the book were counting on me. Down the road, the Mercedes sped as we passed through one dusty little town after another. There were miles and miles of farmland as we made it to San Joaquin Valley. It was once so rich, but much of it lay in-furrow because of the lack of precious water. The ten-year drought caused it to look like a wasteland. It was now foreign and unforgiving, much like you would picture the dust bowl of the 1930s, but still, there were picturesque scenes of beautiful Victorians from better days dotted along the highways. Some places still received water, and their orange groves and wine vineyards were still thriving, but they were sparse. Families at the turn of the century had water contracts that still allowed water for their properties. Sometimes they used them, and other times, they sold them. No matter the case, water was like gold, and if you had it, you were normally rich.

As I looked at Tara, I asked, "Where are you from?"

"Oh, from here and there, mostly there."

"Family?" I asked as my next question, trying to get her to open up. "Not really, not anymore."

"I am sorry. I did not mean to be so flippant."

She sighed. "I am originally from Montreal. Mom is dead, and I don't know where my father is. He left when I was about three. It was just Mom and me. How about you?"

"Both parents are dead. They died in an automobile accident. This car belonged to my mom. It, along with our family's business, was left to me."

"Your mom and dad were detectives?"

"No, palm readers. They were gypsies, believers in magic spells and general mystic going on. So I became interested in the paranormal. I studied it at Berkley."

"So that is why they called you when the book came up missing? I suppose there are others in your field, but, Sterling, you come with a magic background. You grew up with it. Sterling, let's open the book some more.

"More magic, no! It is too dangerous—"

But before I could finish my thought, she had the book in her hands and opened it. A blast of blue light shot out, blinding us. The car began to slide, and I hit the brakes. The car stopped sideways on the side of the road just inches from a large sycamore tree. Reaching for the book and closing it, the new light had blasted into the heavens, scarring the sky above for whatever might have escaped. There was nothing I could see.

"Do you see anything Tara?" She stepped out of the car, holding her eyes as they had not yet readjusted. I got out of the car and went around to where she was standing. I grabbed her by the shoulders. "Let me see your eyes." She seemed all right. She said she was all right. "Are
_ _ _y» you sure?

"Yes, Sterling, I am fine."

"Look, Tara, that is how things are released from the book, by opening it. Sometimes it is good, and sometimes it is not." I searched the skies again but didn't see anything out of the ordinary. I still had the feeling of doom there, and I had to accept this feeling as true.

"Sterling, I am not sorry. That book can make us rich and powerful if we let it."

"Tara, first of all, money and power is not what my ambitions in life are. Yes, money is a necessity to living well, but I do pretty well. As for power, well, power over me is a pretty good start. Now let's keep an eye out for whatever was released from the book."

It didn't take long. As soon as we got back to the car, a blue flash shot by the window so fast we could not make it out whatever it was. Then again, it went by, and this time it rocked the car back and forth from the velocity. Out in the distance, we could see it. It was dark blue with a light blue streak behind it. In a hard pull upward in a giant circle, it was headed back toward us again. It had only buzzed us, so I could not tell if it was good or bad yet.

The blue blur finished its circle and began to match speed with the Mercedes. It was just in front of us, and I could see it was something like an eagle, a very large blue eagle. It had white eyes and blue feathers, and its beak was dark and at least a foot long. The talons looked like giant hooks, and its wingspan was no less than fifteen feet. He looked as if he could literally lift the car. He let out an ear-piercing screech.

"Well, what do you think of your bluebird from the book?" Tara was ready to shoot the bird when it transformed into a birdman, sitting on my hood as we traveled 60 mph. Easing the car off the road, Tara commented, "I like it! That was not such a bad-looking bird!"

The Mercedes rumbled to a stop, and we all just stared at one another for about a minute. Finally, the birdman stood and walked off the car. Tara and I exited the car as well.

The birdman began to speak. "My name is Baltro. You have released me from the book. I grant you life. Now why have you released me?"

"It was kind of an accident," replied Tara. "An accident, it must have been some kind of mistake."

"Yes," I replied in a very cautious voice.

"So you do not know who Baltro is?" the birdman asked.

"No, not really, except you are a giant blue eagle man," Tara said, this time with a nervous laugh.

I asked, "What is it that Baltro does?"

"I am a skin tender."

"Oh no, Sterling, this does not sound good," Tara said as she brought up her Desert Eagle 500.

However, it was too late. Baltro had lunged and grabbed her with one of his large talons. Then with one flap of the large wings, he was airborne. At the same time, I was able to get one shot off that struck his temple. The head shot had done the trick, and Tara and Baltro landed about twenty feet away in a large plume of blue feathers.

Tara was freeing herself, saying something I could not make out. When she stood, two rounds from her big gun sounded out. "Hands off, you freaking overgrown parakeet." She then kicked the birdman and began cursing. The birdman began to turn into a blue candescent light and then was gone. "For real, Sterling, a head shot? I had him right where I wanted him!"

"Where was that, Tara? Halfway between a perch where you were the main course for brunch? Were your skin would have been saved for the skin tender? Are you okay?"

"Yes, I am fine."

"Good to hear. Now don't mess with the book. We may run out of lucky chances."

"You do not have to tell me about the book again!"

In just a few moments, we were on the road again. *Clip clop, clip clop* as the tires rolled across the concrete roadway. We would be coming into Bakersfield soon, and we needed food and fuel. However, we also needed to stay off the grid. We stopped at Jay's truck stop, which also had the Scottsman Inn that would be just the place to hide out for the night. A known hangout for outlaws, bikers, drug dealers, and just bad people, we would fit right in.

It had been a long day and with the rough road and the birdman. Somehow in the back of my mind, I could not stop thinking about the skin tender. All the others had come out of the book together, Perkio and the drogs. Now I wondered, *Is this birdman the only one?*

The Scottsman Inn was near capacity, but we managed to get a room. Once inside, we settled in for some takeout Chinese. We began to talk about what we would do with the book once we had gotten it back to the Brothers of the Suffering Order. Then we talked about her and me for as long as we could, which was not long before we were in each other's arms. Sleep would come soon after our lovemaking, but our sleep was interrupted by fighting and gunshots outside the room. Finally, it calmed down for the night.

At daybreak after a hot shower session, we went to the little cafe at the truck stop. It was a simple breakfast of two eggs, bacon, and toast, along with as much coffee as I could put down. Tara had the short stack of pancakes smothered in butter, syrup, and blueberries, along with one large glass of milk. There was not much talking before we were back on the road by 7:00 a.m. It would be dangerous as we got back onto I-5 South. We passed a lot of grape vineyards as we started up the Tejon Pass; it was a long steep grade between Bakersfield and Los Angeles. The old Mercedes got a little hot, so at the top, we pulled over and let it cool down.

It was beautiful at the top of the pass with its rolling golden mountains. So we took in the beauty surrounding us as I also took in her beauty. It was hard to focus on much of anything else. Her eyes, her smile, her hair, and her body—it was all intoxicating. The more I took in, the more I became off balance. I put my arms around her waist and pulled her close to kiss her.

"As nice as this is, we have a job to do," I said.

"You're right. Let's get it done. Then we can get back to what is important," she said as she kissed me again. We laughed, and then we headed to the car to continue on our journey.

As soon as I settled into the driver's side, lightning flashed a quarter mile away just behind an old stand of walnut trees with about fifteen or sixteen trees as far as I could tell. There were more flashes. I yelled for Tara to get in the car. As I spoke, the trees parted like a cut loaf of bread down the middle. Outstepped a giant Viking or at least what looked like a giant what looked like a Viking. It was running full force toward us.

"Get in!" I yelled again.

The wheels were spinning at full force as Tara shut the door. The giant had a good angle and was covering ground fast. Pulling hard on the steering wheel to avoid the ground, the Mercedes slid sideways into traffic and was hit by an 18-wheeler, which spun the car around. We were right in the path of the giant. Everything looked to be moving in slow motion, and with every spin of the car, it was like watching stop-motion photography. It was one horrific scene after another as the Viking came into view, downward-pointing horns on his helmet and large metal bands around his waist with chains that had spikes. His boots were made of leather and fur with metal rubbing a massive kilt made of bearskin and pinned with the bear head next to him paled in comparison.

In the next still, the giant was lifting a gleaming ten-foot-long silver-and-gold sword above his head as the car completed another side revolution. The sword was cutting the car down the middle with one mighty blow. The car was sliced in half, and at that point, I lost consciousness.

I awoke to a crowd of people trying to release me from the wreckage. The giant and the other half of the Mercedes were gone, along with Tara. After about ninety minutes, I was free from the car. I had some big bruises, but nothing was broken. The people who freed me seemed to think the truck cut the car in half. No one had seen a giant. Standing by what was left of the car, my vision became a little blurry. It was blood from a cut along my hairline. The police and the fire truck were just showing up at the scene.

Where was the twenty-foot giant Viking? I remembered the small grove of walnut trees that he had come out of, and that was where I was going. There was a large 4x4 parked on the side of the road with the door open. Breaking loose from the crowd's hold, the dash to the truck was a shaky one, but I made it. I jumped in and started the car as a man was running and yelling at me. I made a U-turn and headed for the walnut grove, finding a clear path.

Five minutes later, I broke through the grove, finding a clearing. A mile or two in the distance where he was with the other half of the car. The big 4x4 was fast, and it quickly caught up just as he turned and saw the truck on his heels. The truck smashed into his Achilles, and down he went. The second half of the car flew from his hands, but the big 4x4 kept going up his spine till it rammed into the back of his head and neck, causing it to decapitate the giant Viking. *That is for cutting my car in half,* I thought as the head rolled about fifty more yards. Slamming on the brakes, I made a mad dash to what was left of the Mercedes. I could hear Tara's voice calling to get her out of here.

"Okay, hang on! Tara, I am coming!" As I approached the mangled wreckage, it was obvious something was terribly wrong. There was blood covering the shredded metal. As I peered into what was left of the window, I could see Tara's left leg was missing below the knee. Taking off my belt, I quickly made a tourniquet to stop the bleeding.

"Help me through the window, Sterling," she asked in a very calm manner. As I carried her to the truck, she put her arms around my neck. "I knew you would save me."

Once back in the 4x4, we headed back to the scene of the accident. There, I explained what had happened. When the 18-wheeler struck the car, half of it went flying into the woods, and Tara was trapped, and that was the cause of my rash behavior. Everyone seemed to understand, and I grabbed my bag and Tara's knapsack out of what was left of the Mercedes. I climbed into the ambulance. We headed to the hospital, where she spent the next few hours in surgery. The doctor told me that her leg had to be amputated above the knee because of the severity of the wound, that she would be just fine and could go and see her in a few minutes.

She appeared to be sleeping. Leaning over the bed, I took her hand, and for a moment, she opened her eyes. In a slight whisper, she said for me to please take the book home.

"I will, but you have to rest now." Then she fell asleep.

The police questioned me at the hospital about the accident and how the other half of the car was so far away. I explained that there must have been a blowout that had caused the whole thing. Then that going through the woods, the 4x4 must have hooked what was left of the Mercedes. They believed it for the most part. There was no drug or alcohol test needed.

After four more hours, the nurse suggested I go home, clean up, and get some rest. Explaining that we were from out of town, they suggested a motel just around the corner from the hospital. They mentioned it had a small cafe with some pretty good food. Tara would be there for at least seven days. A shower and some food sounded really good, along with some sleep.

The Cottage Inn was not much to look at, but it looked clean. After checking in and taking a shower, I headed to the small cafe. It was mostly empty. They had a row of booths along a large plate-glass window. There was a small stainless steel bar with five stools bolted to the floor. One waitress was filling saltshakers. I seated myself at a booth by the window, and its view gave me a sense of relaxation. The waitress made her way over to me, pulling her order pad from her apron.

"What can I get you?" she asked with a big smile as if she were seeing an old friend. She laid down a plastic folder with today's menu. "Today's special is veal parmesan. You get a house salad and choice of a side. Your choices are baked potato, rice pilaf, or mixed vegetables."

She was really pretty, and I could not help but think she was working beneath herself. Her name tag said "Stephanie." "The veal parmesan with the rice pilaf and a glass of sweet tea. Oh, and may I have a glass of water, Stephanie?"

"Yes, you may," she said with a huge smile as she headed toward the kitchen window.

I was sitting and contemplating the day's events when Stephanie appeared with water, iced tea, and silverware.

"Here you go. Are you with someone at the hospital? We get a lot of family and friends of people in the hospital here."

"Yes, I am with somebody in the hospital."

"I am sorry. I hope they are going to be okay."

"Yeah, me too." Then she headed back to filling the saltshakers.

I couldn't help but feel bad that I had let Tara open the book. I couldn't let it affect me. I had to get this book back to the monastery in St. Rayes. My food came, but I was so tired I did not remember eating it. Leaving Stephanie a good tip, I made my way back to the room. I laid the bag with the book and guns under the bed, and I was out like a light until eight the next morning.

I called the hospital to find out how Tara had faired through the night, and they replied she slept and the doctor would be in about nine in the morning and he could give me a better prognosis. Stopping for coffee, I made my way to the hospital room, where the woman who was trying to kill me a couple of days earlier and now I was checking on her and hoping she would be all right was confined. As I got to the room, the doctor was doing his examination. The nurse met me at the door and told me I would have to wait outside in the waiting room till the doctor was through. She kindly showed me to the door.

After about forty-five minutes, the doctor appeared in the waiting room. "Are you Tara's family?"

"No, we were just traveling together. We were in the wreck together. How is she doing?"

"Right now, she is not out of the woods yet. She has a long road of recovery ahead. Do you know how to get in touch with her family? I am sorry I did not catch your name."

"Sterling Gray, and no, I don't know how or if she even has a family."

"Mr. Gray, you have fifteen minutes with her. Then she will need her rest. She is heavily sedated, so try not to wake her up. Do you understand?"

"Yes, of course. Thank you," I said as I headed toward her room.

She had lines and tubes coming out of her body. She looked thin and frail, not like the dynamo from the day earlier. I thought, *This hospital is in for one hell of a ride when she wakes up.* Standing by the bed, I held her hand and spoke quietly to her, telling her she would be okay and that I was there for her. She must have heard me as she squeezed my hand and tried to say something. I leaned over close to her mouth, and she said, "St. Rayes, go." She squeezed my hand again.

"Okay, I will, and then I will come back for you. All right, my darling?" My answer got no response as she had drifted back to unconsciousness.

ST. RAYES

AFTER RENTING A car from Avis and leaving Bakersfield again, I headed south toward St. Rayes. My thoughts were on Tara. She and I had not talked of who had helped her steal the book and who had given her the information she had needed to locate and remove the book from St. Rayes. It was too late to ask her now. Hopefully, it was an outside influence and none of the Brothers of the Suffering Order.

The traffic was moving at a good track over the grapevine into the Los Angeles basin. The sky was fairly clean today. The wind was coming off the Pacific, blowing the heavy smog out, making for a beautiful day. It was seventy-eight outside and no clouds. If the traffic holds, I should be in St. Rayes by nightfall. The ride was still very long, so I would stop outside San Clemente, California, to grab a bite to eat and stretch my legs.

I called the hospital to check on Tara's condition. It hadn't changed. It suddenly occurred to me Tara and the white light in my dream was the hospital. I had not been paying attention. What else had I missed? Focusing on my vision and what my eyes had seen in it had to be the priority. Right now, it was telling me that it was not going to be safe in St. Rayes.

Around 3:00 p.m., the traffic began to get heavy, but still, the I-5 was moving at a good pace. The people were making their way home from work, school, and everyday commitments, not knowing right next to them on I-5 was an alternative universe. There was magic in a book that was dark and good all in a satchel and just by opening it could unravel their world as it was now. They were listening to their car stereos, talking on their cell phones, or just daydreaming about the upcoming weekend, oblivious to the certain danger close to them. The responsibilities of the guardian of this book were so immense in scope that my mind began to reel. The thought of the power of good and bad was overwhelming. I threw the satchel onto the floorboard of the car and turned the radio up loud to try and distract my current thought pattern.

The temperature outside was near 103 degrees, and perhaps that had something to do with my mind racing. I cranked up the airconditioning. A song from CCR was playing, and for a moment, it took me back to my childhood. That moment was of a much safer and simpler time, sitting on the back of the porch of our home, listening to the radio on a hot summer night, the feverish glow of the heat still rising from the hot sun baking the ground, with nothing to worry about but keeping cool and getting the words right to the songs we heard. I couldn't sing then, and I couldn't sing now, but it was helping detour my mind from Tara and the mission I was on.

The lights of Los Angeles were starting to shimmer. The road was a dull gray with pinstripes. The cars were lining up as far as one could see, and there was a long ribbon of red-and-white taillights. Now there were just splashes of blue, red, gray, black, and silver, or what every color people would fancy to make their car "their car" was now slowly going by in rush-hour traffic. It looked and felt like you were stuck in a never-ending river that slowly flowed to the ocean. As soon as the exit for Newport Beach was passed by, the traffic began opening up toward San Diego. Another couple of hours and I would be at St. Rayes. The right side of the car began to show the darkness from the Pacific Ocean.

Calling the hospital, checking on Tara, I was told she was resting comfortably. I was then back up to speed, and the temperatures were still in the eighties. I rolled down the window for some fresh air, if there was such a thing in Southern California with its brown layer of freeway smog. I was in luck, though, because the wind had been blowing, and I could smell and taste the Pacific Ocean. The salt from the breaking waves on the beach and you could almost hear them rolling along the coastline, inviting you to come and get in. The ocean wants you to look to where you first came and will never let you feel as if it is uninviting.

It, however, was the most dangerous place in the world I would suppose from some different perspectives—the sailor at sea with a full shipload and sixty-foot waves smashing into the ship or the shallow straits with fog and jagged rocks; the sea creatures such as the great whites, giant squids, and cephalopods that could crush a small sailing vessel with their thirty-foot tentacles and a two-tone body; and then there are the electric eels and a whole world of poisonous fish that are stinging, biting, and stabbing you. However, still, millions of humans every day go to and get into our beloved oceans. I too personally love the ocean, and after this job, I am going to take Tara to the ocean, where she can recover and just take life easy. It will be the sun, surf, and beer. Tara would have to love beer with her personality and all. I made a mental note to ask Tara if she liked beer.

The sign said 110 miles to St. Rayes, which meant I would get there in about two hours or about nine fifteen at night. I was not sure if the Brothers of Sorrow would be up, but if not, I was sure they would be glad to awaken to be reunited with the book. *The funny thing,* I thought, *is that in all this time of following and chasing the book, I do not know its title. Perhaps it is called the* Witching Hour, *or* Magic Gone Wrong, *possibly even* Conjure This. It may be printed on the book, but I would have to wait until St. Rayes because I sure as hell did not need another adventure if it accidentally opened.

San Diego was 60 miles away, and traffic was light for a Wednesday. Everybody had gotten home early. As I got closer, I could not help but think about Mortrok, Li Chen, and Esmeralda and wonder if I would ever see them again. Maybe the Brothers of the Suffering Order would know how to bring them out of the book safely. I thought they would be waiting for me when I arrived, but I knew that was wishful thinking. However, after the week I had, it would not surprise me if they were waiting. Making good time, I would be there as soon as the lights of San Diego were in sight. Gleaming like a thousand stars, San Diego was truly a diamond for California's collection of beautiful cities. I-5 cut down the middle of it like a jeweler cut on a precious stone.

The town of St. Rayes was four miles away, and there were a lot of questions that needed to be answered. I was not sure that I was the one to ask them. Just getting the book back seemed like a big effort for me. I thought could I just drop the book off, get paid, and be on my way. I truly didn't think so.

I took the Rayes turn off the highway, and soon after, the monastery came into view. There were only two lights on in the entire complex. I parked the rental car in adjacent parking, which was very small but adequate to park the rental car. As I sat in the parked car for a moment, it was eerily silent. There was the pale yellow hue of the light shining off the building. I grabbed the satchel with the book and began to make my way slowly across the parking lot.

At the monastery, each step I took felt heavy on my soul. The large wooden doors with their iron hinges easily pushed open. The doors led to a smaller foyer, which was not lit by the light. Walking just a few more feet into the moving sanctuary, an almost inaudible bell rang out at 10:00 p.m. The bell was muted for sleeping purposes, but still, the sound was chilling. At the front of the altar, there was a priest lighting candles. As I walked closer, he turned around and saw who I was.

"Mr. Gray." He embellished. It was Abbot Noland. "Do you have the book, Mr. Gray?" he said as he turned from lighting the candles and hurried my way. The candles shone off his head to the point where I could not distinguish his head from the candlelight. His head and face all but disappeared into the silhouette of the flickering light. The all-day drive could have also been affecting my vision.

"Yes, I have the book right here," I said as I fished around the satchel to return it. He held out his hands eagerly like a child waiting for an ice cream cone. "Not so fast, Abbot. What about my money, and there are a couple of extra expenditures we need to talk about such as my car being cut in half by a giant Viking?"

"Mr. Gray, you have done a phenomenal job, and you will be compensated for all your troubles. Now may I see the book?"

"Yes, of course."

Handing him the book, he rubbed it as if it were a picture of a long-lost relative. Then to my surprise, he opened the book. My first reaction was to duck, but there was no light, no shattering moments, no giant beast from the underworld, any wizards or witches, or voodoo kings. There was nothing, and my thoughts came across loud and clear.

"You were expecting something from the book, yes?" the Abbot asked as if he knew the answer already. "Magic, but you see, Mr. Gray, I am not a reader of this book. If I were to read the book, all I would get is a lot of worlds that make up a fantastic story of adventure, magic, and characters with powers beyond belief, dark tales of the struggles between good and evil, love and hate, and betrayal of the mind and heart. You see, it is you, Sterling Gray, who brings the story to life in this world."

"No disrespect, Abbot, but that is the craziest thing I have ever heard in my life. There has been creature after creature and person after person who was as real as you and me, Abbot. There has been death, magic, bombs, love, monsters, time, and travel, and not only have I seen it. I have felt it. It's real."

"Of course, it was real. You are a reader like your mother was a reader. That is how you have the power to make this book real. Anything in the book, including what you write, you can make it real."

"Let me get this straight. You're saying all the things that have happened is because I read the book, this book right here, and that anything inside, I am able to make it become real?"

"Yes, that is correct except that you don't have to really read the book. As long as you have the book, you, Mr. Gray, can make up your own stories, such as Mortrok," he said, and then Mortrok appeared next to the abbot.

"Hello, Sterling," Mortrok said as he raised his eyes from his smoky gray hat. A big smile came across my face.

I moved close as I put my hand on Mortrok's shoulder. "Is everything all right with you and the book?"

"Yes, Sterling, everything is all right now that we are here."

"How about Esmeralda?" I asked.

"She is fine, but ask her yourself." And on the opposite side of the pulpit, just behind the abbot, she appeared in her purple mist as beautiful and desirable as ever.

I quickly moved to her and took her hand. "Sterling, you handsome, brave man. You have returned the book safely. There is something more you wish to tell me, and it is of love. You are in love, that is it? Yes, you are in love with a girl."

"Yes, I am in love with a girl, the girl who stole the book, and she stole my heart."

"You mean Tara Jones?"

"Yes, that is who I mean. She is back in Bakersfield in the hospital. So I must hurry to return, but first, I wanted to see all of you and tell you how much you mean to me."

"Sterling, we know how much we mean to you," a voice said from the front row seats in the pew. It was Li Chen, my voodoo general from

China. Again, I was overwhelmed with joy to know he was safe and here to greet me.

"The book has brought me here with you and has shown me what your lives have been and who you are. The book has also shown me how to be brave in the face of adversity, how to understand that I also have magic within me, and given me a vision of who I can become. I now have a compass of where I am to go."

The wind began to move suddenly above our heads, and a loud flapping noise and a shrill of laughter were heard as the blue birdman landed on the chain in the corner of the church. Instincts told me to reach for my gun.

"No, wait, Sterling," Esmeralda said. "Use your mind, for it is you that has released the birdman."

"How is that possible? I killed him. He is dead."

The birdman laughed again. "You must really like me to bring me back again," he said, followed by another insidious laugh. Two large drogs appeared on both sides of the room with blue flames dripping from their mouths. The one on the right spewed out a little pool of blue flame, igniting the wall and some of the seats. The one on the left sent a large plume into the air of blue flames everywhere, and out of the middle of it, here came Perkio.

"I see I have made it back, Sterling, and I intend to rule the world."

"You will rule nothing," Mortrok said. "Stewy is the reader of the book and the author of the book if he so wishes."

The building began to rumble and shake as one of the walls caved in from the force of a rolla rolling through the wall and standing at least ten feet tall.

"What is going on here?" I asked.

"It is you, Sterling. You are composing or returning in the book a chapter you may have in your head. You may be reading right now in your mind, but whatever it is, it is about to get real," Li Chen said as he stood and began to yell out an incantation.

Things were starting to move in slow motion for me. Through the hole in the wall in stepped the Viking.

"Oh, my beloved birdman, you are alive."

"Yes, it seems our old friend Sterling could not live without us."

"So true. It would be a human to assemble us for your pleasure. Well, when you put it that way, no!" The giant Viking lifted his giant sword above his head as if he were summoning all the power from all the evil Viking gods he could and, in one downward, sliced three rows of seating in the pews. "Well, let's play," he said as he brought the sword above his head again.

Mortrok raised both of his hands and yelled, "Alto manifold!" and the giant Viking soon stopped right in his tracks. "Sterling, my magic will not hold him very long."

Perkio floated around the room, and with a wave of his hands, the drogs spit out more blue flames. Esmeralda moved with lightning speed, leaving a purple mist behind her and momentarily blinding Perkio and his drogs. Then there was the sickening sound of the rolla shifting his shape into a boulder. The floor beneath him gave way as he began turning and churning like a giant ship propeller, chopping and grinding gaps in the floor.

"Sterling, we cannot hold them! You must do something!" Li Chen said.

I grabbed the book from the abbot and started back toward the doors. I was not sure what it was I was supposed to do. I held the book above my head and yelled, "Stop, all of you! Just stop!" Then for a split second, they all did. Everyone and everything stopped, and they all just looked at me.

Then all hell broke out. The rolla whizzed past at neck-breaking speed, cutting through the floor like a hot knife through butter, rolling over the abbot, and just missing me. It tried to stop, but its momentum carried it straight through the wall. I could feel the heat of a blast of the hot blue flame pass just behind my head, which lit more church pews. Li Chen yelled more as the Viking threw a sweeping chop with his gigantic sword. Small pieces of hail fell from my head. The giant Viking loaded another wild swing. A magical blast from Mortrok knocked the giant backward but not off his feet. Esmeralda began to fill the room with her purple mist just as the birdman grabbed her. They both disappeared into thin air, and a few moments later, Esmeralda reappeared without the birdman. She smiled ever so slightly. I hoped she had dropped him off in some small birdcage far, far away. The Viking, noticing what had happened, turned his attention toward Esmeralda.

"Bring back my birdman, witch!"

He swung the sword wildly in her direction, and again, Mortrok fired a magic blast at him and this time using two hands. The thundering blast struck him in the back of head, launching him forward and onto his sword. The giant Viking was on his hands and knees as if he were praying. The blade struck a few feet out of his back. There was green pus running out of his putrid soul.

There was hardly any time to think as the rolla came crashing through the wall. The dynamic pile of rocks crushed everything in its path. I had to move, and I had to move fast. Again, I moved in just the nick of time like a matador. The big rock was not nimble and moved right past me. He went across the floor, trying to change the rotation he was spinning, but it was too late. He went straight through another wall.

Li Chen held Perkio, but he was starting to lose his hold on him. I was back to my feet; however, a drog leaped at me. I fell to the floor again in a near miss. St. Rayes was being demolished. The drog hit the wall just as the rolla came through it. Blue blood gushed like Jell-O, and again, I rolled out of the way. The rolla continued right over the pulpit and through the back wall. It was clear to me that the rolla had no line of sight. It could not see where it was rolling. The second drog was after me, and I ran to where the Viking lay slumped over with his massive sword. *This has to work, or I would die,* I thought. The drog squared off in front of me with his large tail wagging back and forth. Angrily, he crouched and then leaped. Falling to the floor, I kicked with both legs, launching the dragon toward the drog during his trajectory toward me to his death as he landed on the dead Viking's sword. As it was impaled on the sword, it let out a bloodcurdling screech that dulled any other sound in the room. Perkio erupted like a volcano. The blue flames filled the corner of the church. Li Chen was hurled across the room, smashing into a wall. He crumpled to the floor. Perkio sprang through the room with fire from both hands. If there was something that was not on fire, it was now, including me. Remembering stop, drop, and roll from kindergarten, that was what I did. Esmeralda crossed back and forth, leaving a purple mist, blinding everyone in the room.

Mortrok yelled, "Sterling, do you still have the book!" Yelling back into the mist, he said, "Open it and command Perkio back in the book!

You can do it! It is our only chance!"

Opening the book, I commanded Perkio to go back into the book. "You are too weak. I am not going back into the book."

"Do not listen to him, Sterling! You can do this! You are the reader and the writer of this book!"

Again, I commanded Perkio into the book. Nothing happened, and the rolla blasted through the wall, and this time he stood. You could almost see him breathing. He walked slowly toward Mortrok, and then he stopped just in front of him. He pointed at Perkio, and with a deep canyon sound, he simply said, "Hurting rolla!"

Perkio turned his attention to the rolla, sending blue flames blazing toward the giant rock man. He began to glow red from the blue flames. Mortrok hit Perkio again with a powerful magic blast.

"Now, Sterling, command him back into the book! You are the great descendant of Giloc! That is how you are able to read and control the book!"

"Perkio, back to your pages, back to the cell which is your destiny!" Perkio began to fade, and the flames stopped burning as he did. The rolla grabbed him, and he also began to fade. Perkio just stared as he was being crushed, and soon, they were both gone. The room was still burning, and most of the building was demolished.

Esmeralda floated down beside Mortrok. "You've done it. Sterling, you sent them all back," Esmeralda said. "You are descendant of Giloc. Now give us the book so we all can return to it in peace."

The doors behind me opened slowly, and in walked Tara Jones with both her legs. "Hello, Esmeralda, Mortrok. Hello, Sterling, my beloved."

"Tara, how is this possible? I left you in Bakersfield in the hospital with only one leg."

With that, she pulled out a TIG Series Desert Eagle and said, "Sterling, give me the book! This, my love, is evil. You see, all of us in the book are evil—Perkio, the Viking, and the birdman. Oh, and yes, Esmeralda, Li Chen, and Mortrok are all evil as am I. The plan was we would get out of the book in order to rain down our malevolence and our immoral disparity on mankind. Your great-great-great ancestor, Giloc, locked us away one by one, and it had taken us four hundred years to get here, outside of the book. Without you, we were imprisoned in the book. We all must go back to our quarantine cells in the pages of the book. So I will take that book," as she grabbed it from my hand at the gunpoint.

"Very Tara," Mortrok said with a smile. "Now give me the book so I may imprison him forever."

"Not so fast, Mortrok," Tara Jones said with more than a little authority. "Do you see this satchel here? It contains ten pounds of C4 explosives. So nobody moves because with that much explosive, I can blow up the book, the building, and everyone in it."

"This is not part of the plan, Tara. You know Sterling must be placed in the book as soon as possible," Esmeralda said to Tara.

"Yes, I know, but that is no longer part of the plan. That is not going to happen now. You see, somewhere between Stockton and Bakersfield, I fell in love with Sterling Gray. I don't know how, but I did."

Mortrok and Esmeralda transformed from the kind, caring souls I had come to know to the demonic creatures they truly were from the book.

"Now, Tara Jones, maybe you can change so Stewy here can see the real you," Mortrok said with the charted sounds of his demon voice.

"Yes," Esmeralda chimed in with her screech of a voice, barely audible to human standards.

"It was no wonder that Giloc put you two in the evil book. Just listen to you. The world couldn't possibly take that such bad vitriol that spews from your mouths. To think I was so worried about my newfound friends."

"It is just power, Sterling, and whoever has it, she will rule the worlds," screeched Esmeralda.

"Esmeralda!" Mortrok said. "We can rule the worlds together, right, Li Chen?"

"Right, we shall rule together."

"No, we shall not rule together," Tara said. "We shall burn together in the book," she said as she turned to me. "It is time for me to end this demonstrative experiment. Sterling, I love you so much, and that is why I must do this."

"No, Tara, you do not have to do this. Please, I love you too, please!"

She smiled while staring deep into my eyes, and then with a front kick that had the force of a mule, she kicked me in my chest, knocking me through the church doors and beyond some twenty feet. I rolled another fifteen feet or so, and the last thing I could remember was the church doors closing, and there was a bright light.

EPILOGUE

HEY! WAKE UP! Come on! Wake up!"

Slowly opening my eyes, I felt the hot kiss of the sunlight on my cheek, the wet dew on the tall grass in which I was lying in. The blue sky with puffs of white clouds almost motionless was passing over my head. Then there was a hard poke in my chest.

"Are you okay?" the red mass of hair with big eyes leaning over me asked. "Come on, Sleeping Beauty, rise and shine." It was some kind of police officer.

I pushed to the ground onto my elbows to better get my bearings of where I was, and there in front of me were the ruins of the monastery.

Only the foundation was partially remaining. "Where is it?" I asked.

"Where is what? The old church? It has been gone for forty or fifty years. There was some kind of fire, I think," she replied.

"But I was just inside a few minutes ago," I said, bewildered.

"Well, first of all, there is not much to be inside of, and you have been lying here for about twenty minutes. Look around, there is nobody else here that I can see. Come on now, and let's get up and get you out of here. You are not supposed to be here. This place has been condemned for years, and I could write you a ticket for being here."

Making it to my feet, I slowly surveyed the area, and there was nothing, just ruins. I patted down my head and body to make sure everything was still there. I turned around and noticed my Mercedes was parked just behind us.

"That is a nice car you have there."

"Thanks," I managed to murmur. I dragged my hand along the hood of the car till I reached the door. The keys were in the ignition.

"Are you sure you are okay to drive?"

"Yeah, I am fine. Thank you," I said, sitting for a moment in the car, looking out at the hood. Was this just a summer's dream, or was I losing my mind? I started the car and tapped on the window while pushing the button to let it down. Officer Stephanie, with her bug-eyed glasses, peered into the window. I felt a little odd that her name and the waitress's back at the little restaurant were both the same and they both had red hair.

"Okay, are you sure you are good and can make it back to the main road?"

"Oh yeah, no problem. Guess I just needed a little nap, but have a great day, Officer," I said.

I backed the Mercedes into a half circle, turning toward the main highway. Checking the rearview mirror, she stood tall in the road, watching as I drove away. My mind started to race. What had happened to Tara Jones, Mortrok, and the others? St. Rayes had been gone for decades. Was it gone at all, or was it just some magic spell cast over it to make it look as if it were gone? The book, it must have been real. There was just too much for it not to be. My feelings for Tara felt so real and that she had become and was part of my life.

The Mercedes rolled silently along the highway, and I could feel the morning sun burning my face as it filled the inside of the Mercedes with a bright glare. Along my right, I-5 was coming into view, and I would make the turn north toward my home. I still kept thinking maybe, just maybe, some sense could be made of this. The traffic was quiet, silent, even though it was passing by my window alongside me. The cars, trucks, and life itself felt like it was passing by. I sped the Mercedes up to match the world outside. Inside the car, everything was at a stop— no wind, no motion—almost like a picture. A snapshot of a point in time that had already played out and I was looking at some pictures of my life. First, there was San Diego and then LA like one picture after another. I was headed up to I-5 to the hot San Joaquin Valley, but first, I drove through Bakersfield and then Fresno and Madera, California. I stopped for fuel and food, and in another few hours, I would be home. My brain was starting to spin from a false sense of beauty and was making things even worse. I was beginning to hear voices. The voices in my head were familiar voices. They were kind of far off in the distance, over and over, but I could not make out who it was or what they were saying. Traffic began in slow motion. The occasional face might be watching me as they went by, staring as if to look inside my soul. There was a woman, a child, and they were just staring as if they were looking at a picture, some picture of what was happening to me. Was it consciousness, self-awareness, or obliviousness to the true reality of my own state, and what was this obsession with holding on to just one thing, one person, and one scrap of my life?

Then a truck appeared out of nowhere, crushing the Mercedes like an aluminum can under one's foot. The wreckage was scattered for about a fourth of a mile. In the ambulance, I could hear that no one was sure of what color the car was. There just were not enough pieces to tell for sure. They said almost all my 206 bones may be broken. The attendant in the ambulance was saying, "He is back again!" Back from where, and how many times had I already come back? There was light again and the voices in my head. What the hell was going on? There was no pain, and I was not scared. I was actually feeling comfortable and at ease. There was something even familiar about the voices.

There was then a blinding light in one eye, and I tried to focus on what I could see, but even before I could, there was a searing pain in my eye. I was unable to scream, and my other eye was opened to the white flash, and the searing pain was back. They would continue to open my eye, and I was thinking they were going to burn out of my head. Feeling the blood run down my face was mortifying, and then it struck me. It was not blood; it was tears. They were cool as they ran down my cheek and into my ears as they had done a hundred times before when I was a child. The voices became more distinct. The rhythm and cadence were a standard embedded in the very fabric of my soul. Those voices were my mommy and daddy, talking around me as they had when I was six or seven. They were talking to each other in a way that as a child, I could learn and understand what they were saying or knowing it was for my benefit, the reassurance from one of their smiles or the particular glances from my pops with a raised eyebrow as to say "You get it, don't you?" and I did. Usually, it made me a little more confident and allowed me to feel as if I stood a little taller in their eyes, growing from their nurturing of their seed. They were always watching out for me, even when Mom let me take her 1969 Mercedes to the store eighteen months earlier, when the 18-wheeler had run over me, shattering not only my life but theirs as well.

Listening to them talk and move about the room, it was all coming back now—the wreck, the bones mending, and the sounds of the voices day after day and my mother's tears on my face as she wept for her baby and my father agonizing at the pain of his childhood in a place where he could just be there and wait for as long as it took, which could be days, months, or years. He would continue to be my father and see to my needs. He would wash me and turn my body a couple of times every day. Once the cast was off, he began the day-to-day physical therapy that would be needed to keep me from becoming completely useless. He read me story after story just as he did when I was a child. Stories were of the good warlock and evil witches, Viking giant, voodoo kings, and the Chinese emperor with dogs like dragons for allies, who just happened to have blue flames. There were beautiful women such as Esmeralda, a spellbinding witch who, with just her essence, could make you fall head over heels in love with her, and there was a woman like Tara Jones, who, with her strength and her sheer beautiful presence, was able to capture my heart and soul for life. They were there in the book my father had been reading to me for the past year and a half as I lay in bed like a vegetable. It was strange my body was not working, but my mind was coming back into focus, and it was all frightening and terrifying for sure. I would have gone mad had it not been for these voices, their touch, and most of all, their stories that let my mind have a place to go and be safe, some picture of what my life may have been.

"Well, what have we here for you today? A story about a boy and a dragon's adventures here on earth and the celestial by Arthur C. Jett," my pops said with some enthusiasm. "All I could think about was how I am supposed to breathe in space!" He went on to say "It has a really pretty picture on the front cover," and he opened one of my eyes to show me the dragon flying over a lush green forest with ten thousand stars in the sky. It was spectacular. My eye darted back and forth at the sight of the picture, and then I heard my dad yell.

"It is moving! His eye is moving! Quick, come to see, Mother, his eye is moving!"

My mom came to see. "Quick! Go get the doctor!"

My eye stopped moving as I looked at my mother's face.

She said, "Sterling, if you can see or hear me, try moving your eyes."

I blinked once, and she began to cry uncontrollably. The doctor examined me, and we worked out a code, blink one for yes and two for no. Finally, we got to the water and some small ice chips that were allowed.

I was gasping for anything that sounded like a word. It was "thanks," it is all I could do to get it out, but after that, I started talking, eating, and moving toward a full recovery.

I was overwhelmed that my parents weren't dead. It had just been a manifestation of my mind's defenses to protect it from the dark depths of the psyche. It was not too long before things were back to normal. Work was going just fine with a lot of work from Berkley University on paranormal studies and some houses that needed to be swept. Old houses hosting entities from the beyond and I was more than happy to be back at it. Tara Jones remained on my mind despite being a character from the book. She still seemed so real. It was not normal that the bond between us was so strong. I could still feel her soft skin and her radiant warmth, and her kiss still lingered on my lips. The faint passing wind that carried a scent like hers would turn my head every time. It occurred to me to finish the book that my father had read to me with Tara Jones as a character. When I asked about that particular book, he could not recall any book that had a character Tara Jones in it. After ninety-eight minutes, he could only remember four books that he had read. I headed to the library and checked out some books my pops had, and sure enough, I found the book with Mortrok, Esmeralda, Li Chen, the rolla, and a giant Viking, but there was no Tara Jones.

Being so drawn to her was bad, but knowing that she was just a fictional character in some sci-fi book pushed me to find the reason Tara Jones was on my mind. After searching to no avail, I knew she had to still be somewhere. Was she a client or maybe a nurse? Somehow there was a connection of some kind I needed to find. I googled Tara Jones, and as no big surprise, over eighty matching names came up just in the San Francisco area alone. Narrowing the search to photos and ages, I was able to find her. Tara Jones, twenty-eight, on Cherry Hill Road. She had a profile picture of her in motorcycle leather and MMA as clear as day. There she was in the picture just as she had been in my mind. Getting in my car as fast as I could, I headed for Cherry Hill Road. After about a block, I realized I had no actual address or phone number. According to Google Maps, it was only two blocks total to Cherry Hill Road, and if I had to, I would knock on every door on the street to find her. The street was mostly housing and was going quickly as I worked to find her. Halfway up the hill, it became row houses and duplexes. As luck would have it, the second duplex's first door read Tara Jones. The duplexes were over garages, which made sense as far as her motorcycle being in one. Knocking on her door, there was no answer. I knocked again, this time very loudly.

The next-door neighbor, an elderly woman, came to her door and said, "She is not home and might not ever be back."

"Well, did she move?" I asked politely.

"Are you a family member or a friend?" she asked cautiously.

"No, not really, more of an acquaintance that she had helped in the past."

"Well, I do not see what it would hurt to tell you. She is such a nice girl, and you look like a nice man. Tara is at Bay Memorial Hospital. She has been there for about a year now in a coma. She had an injury from a bad motorcycle accident."

I could not believe what I was hearing. Bay Memorial was the hospital I was in. The woman went on to say that Tara's family had owned the duplex and had not had the heart to lease out her place. I thanked her and jumped in the car and headed for Bay Memorial Hospital. The fourth floor of the hospital was dedicated to long-term trauma victims. Sure enough, there she was, on the ledger for patients in room 402. The nurse at the front desk said without family permission, I could not see her but that some of her family was here now visiting. Maybe I could speak to them and that she would check for me. Soon, a woman in her mid-fifties came to the desk with the nurse. She introduced herself as Mrs. Jones, Tara's mother. In my dream, Tara had no mother or father. "May I help you, young man?"

"Yes, Tara and I are friends. My name is Sterling Gray, and I thought that I might see her."

"Mr. Gray?"

"Please call me Sterling."

"Okay then, Sterling. I do not see what harm that would be with you being a friend and all."

"Thank you, Mrs. Jones."

We headed toward room 402. As we entered, there was a man in the room.

"Sterling Gray, this is my husband, Terrance. Sterling is a friend of Tara," said Mrs. Jones as she introduced me.

"You are friends? I must apologize I don't remember Tara ever speaking of anyone named Sterling."

"No, sir, you would not have. This is going to sound strange, but we met here in the hospital."

"You have been here in my daughter's room before?"

"No, she was in mine. You see, until six months ago, I was a patient here in the hospital. I too was in a coma, and my parents would come and three or four times per week to take care of me. They would read to me to make me part of the conversation. While I was in a coma, I met Tara, and as absurd as that may sound, it is true, and I can prove it. While in my unconscious state, it was dark at first, but my dad read to me, and I began to be part of the story. In those stories, Tara joined me. However, when I went back to find her in the stories, she was not in any of the books. You see, I, I mean, we fell in love in the story, and I could not shake the feeling that she was not just a fictional character in a book. I felt drawn to her still, and as a detective, my investigation led me back to this hospital. She looks just like who I saw in my dreams. She was a strong, opinionated, athletic, and with a mind of her own. She was confident, loyal to a fault. Her courage is why I am alive today. She is loving and the most beautiful woman I have ever known. She pulled me out of the death of my own mind, and now I am here to do the same for her with your permission, of course."

The two of them looked at each other for a long moment. Then Mr. Jones said, "Although your words are very kind, Tara has not moved a muscle in over a year. Everything is done for her. She does not drink on her own, and she cannot go to the bathroom on her own. We roll her over every day, bathe her, and comb her hair. We do it all, and what you are saying is unbelievable."

"Mr. and Mrs. Jones, all I am asking is a chance to prove I am right that she is in there and she wants out."

They looked at each other for a long moment again, and then Mrs. Jones said, "Okay, Sterling, what is it you want to do?"

"I would just like to talk to her for a few moments."

"Just talk?"

"Right, yes."

She nodded yes, and I sat on the side of the bed. I put both my arms on both sides and leaned down close to her. "It is me, Sterling. I am here for you, darling. I am here as long as you need me to be. Tara, I love you. If there is any way that you can let us know you are in there, please, my love, let us know. Tara, I love you."

I rose back off the bed as we got our sign; one single tear rolled down her cheek.

The End

Thank you to God for all my blessings.
Arthur C. Jett